C.K. BushNELL

Printed in the United States of America

Print ISBN: 978-1951490720
E-Book ISBN: 978-1951490737

Canoe Tree
Press

4697 Main Street
Manchester Center, VT 05255

Canoe Tree Press is a division of DartFrog Books.

TABLE OF CONTENTS

Thank you to my son, for begging me to write *Summer Camp Academy*, and giving me his expert advice along the way.

CHAPTER 1
HOW TO RUIN SUMMER

If you want to know how to ruin summer, just ask my parents. They're experts.

I don't think they want to ruin summer. They just can't help it. Last summer, my parents said we were going to take a road trip around the country and go to lots of fun places.

"Yay! Every theme park and water park in the country!" I screamed.

Wrong. We didn't go to any theme parks, amusement parks, water parks, or even an old roller-skating rink. Instead, we went to every science museum, art museum, natural history museum, and library on the east coast, because that is "fun" to my parents. It was the worst summer ever.

Wait, no, it wasn't. The year before, they said we were going to spend the summer in Maine.

"Yay! I'm going to the beach every day! I'm going to build sandcastles, and find pirate treasure!" I declared.

Wrong. We spent the entire time on my great-grandparents' farm doing really hard work. I mean, really hard work. We had to clean out their animal barns and pick vegetables . . . and they had a lot of vegetables.

My name is Noah Benton. I don't know what I want to be when I grow up, but I know I don't want to own a farm. Who wants to clean up animal poop while your friends are swimming in a pool and eating ice cream all day long? But what do I know? I'm only ten. (That's what my parents keep telling me, in case I forget.)

All during the school year, I was waiting for summer. Even though summer has never really worked out the way I wanted it to, I still had high hopes that this year would be different. But my parents went ahead and ruined summer again. Here's how: they said those two scary, horrible words that you should never ever say together: "Summer" and "School."

"Summer School." That's the same as saying: "Summer CANCELED."

Try to imagine being told that your summer has been canceled.

"I'd rather pick weeds! I'd rather go to a museum!" I cried. "You can't do this to me! Summer school is the worst!"

My parents looked at each other and smiled.

"It's not summer school," said Mom. "It's called Summer Camp Academy. It's a fun summer camp deep in the forests of New Hampshire." (Please notice that she said the word "fun.")

"What?" I cried. "Who would ruin a camp by calling it 'Academy'?"

Dad held up a brochure. "It looks great! See all the log cabins and trees!"

I took the pamphlet from my dad and glanced at the pictures. There were kids in canoes, kids around a campfire, kids climbing boulders in hiking gear. "Um . . ."

"I wish I could go there!" Mom said.

"Maybe you should," I whimpered.

Dad read the cover page. "Where kids learn to camp for real."

"Learn?" I didn't get it.

Mom tilted her head and smiled the way she does when she thinks I'm being cute. "Oh, honey, the camp wants to teach you great outdoor activities: how to build your own tent, how to make a fire . . . stuff like that."

"Stuff like that" sounded a lot like spelling tests and times-table flash cards. "But why can't I stay home with you guys?" I stared at a picture of a kid holding a bow and arrow.

"And do what? All your friends are going to camp."

How did my parents know that? I didn't even know that.

"I don't care. I'm not going. It looks horrible." I put on my best pouty face. I could start fake crying if I had to.

My parents were ruining everything. My plan was to hang out with the guys, play kick ball, swim in Josh's pool, and go to the beach. Why couldn't I have a FUN summer For ONCE???

Mom put her arm around me. "Listen, if you really don't like it, you can call us at the end of the week, and we'll come and get you. Okay? But I think you're going to love it."

I frowned some more. "But I'm supposed to have a VACATION between fourth and fifth grade. It's the law or something."

Dad squinted his eyes and rubbed his chin. (He always does that. He's a lawyer.) "I don't think it's the law, but—"

"This will be the best vacation ever. You'll see," said Mom.

CHAPTER 2
WELCOME TO SUMMER CAMP ACADEMY

The big wooden sign deep in the forest read: "SUMMER CAMP ACADEMY—WHERE KIDS LEARN TO CAMP FOR REAL**Z**." Someone had spray-painted the letter "Z" at the end of "real," and the camp just left it that way. I might have liked the sign, too, if it hadn't been for the word "LEARN" in big white letters. Either my parents knew this was really a summer school and weren't telling me, or they honestly didn't know that you weren't supposed to be learning anything during the summer.

The dirt road through the pine trees went on for about five miles. I don't really know how long the road was because the distance to the camp was posted in kilometers. I guess the camp didn't want people to know how long of a drive they were in for. Our science teachers keep trying to make the metric system happen, but it's not happening.

Finally, we got to this big, open area, where there were lots of cars and families swarming around. I didn't want to get out of the car—it looked crazy out there. I mean, really crazy. And there was crying—a lot of crying. Near a wide, dirt pathway leading up to a big, brown cabin was an ever-growing pile of duffle bags and sleeping bags. Parents were lugging these bags out of their cars and heaving them onto this pile. Some of the kids were throwing themselves onto their bags, crying, or trying to pull the bags back out of the pile. It didn't look good. It did not look good. Did these kids already know what they were in for? Or were they just afraid, like I was, that this camp was really a summer school, far away in New Hampshire, where your parents couldn't hear you complaining?

My parents were standing outside the car, waving for me to come out. They were smiling and giving me the thumbs up.

"It's so beautiful here!" Mom announced.

"Oh, to be a kid again!" Dad yelled. "Just look at this place!"

There was a skinny kid with glasses standing right behind my parents with his arms crossed. He was scowling at his parents.

"Harrison, let's go," his mother said.

"You said if I got a C-minus in math, I didn't have to go here," said Harrison.

"No, I said if you got a C-minus or lower you *did* have to go here," his mother replied. She had her arms crossed, too.

Harrison's father was just standing there, juggling the duffle bag and sleeping bag.

I crossed my arms and glared at my parents. I knew they could hear Harrison. They were pretending that they couldn't.

"Come on, buddy!" Dad said.

So this was how they were going to play it—never admit that Summer Camp Academy was summer school. I'd been tricked out of summer again.

I grabbed my lucky yo-yo (how could I forget that?) and climbed out of the car. My lucky yo-yo is red and used to light up, but stopped doing that a while ago. It's been with me since second grade. It's been with me for weed picking at my great-grand-parents' farm; it's been to all the Smithsonian museums—it's even been sent to the principal's office twice for "disrupting the class." Now it would have to get me through so-called camp.

My parents walked along either side of me as we made our way through the maze of cars and crying kids (I wasn't crying—for realz). There was a group of counselors standing in front of the heap of duffle bags holding clipboards. There were about twenty of them, and they all looked like they were in college. They also had big signs hanging around their necks.

My father heaved my duffle bag onto the pile. Then my mother carefully balanced my sleeping bag on top. It looked like they were building a bonfire.

One of the counselors walked right up to me and shook my hand. "Hi, I'm Dev," he said. The sign he was wearing said: "Hi, I'm Dev. River Otters. Fifth Grade Boys."

I shook his hand but didn't say anything.

"You must be Noah Benton," he said.

"Yeah," I said, wondering how he knew that.

He must have known what I was thinking because then he turned his clipboard around to show me a list of boys' names with their pictures. Then he pulled a nametag sticker out of his pocket with "NOAH" written in thick, black marker and handed it to me. I was about to stuff it in my pocket when my mother took it from me.

"Oh, that's a great idea," she said, sticking it in the center of my t-shirt.

That's when another kid came up to Dev with his mother.

"Hi, Walter," Dev said, handing him a sticker.

The kid took one look at the sticker and tossed it on the ground. "My name's Chip," he said.

Dev pulled another name sticker out of his pocket and wrote "Chip," then handed it to Chip.

Chip tossed that one as well. "I'm not wearing this," he said.

Chip's mother looked nervously from Dev to the stickers, now lying on the ground. "Oh, but you have to. I'm sure it's required for security purposes." She picked up the "Chip" sticker.

"No," said Dev. "We just want the campers to get to know each other."

Chip's mother glared at Dev like he needed to play along.

"And for security purposes," he said quickly.

Chip took the dirty sticker and put it on, but way at the bottom of his Red Sox baseball jersey. Chip had light brown hair, like mine, but his hair kind of flipped up at the front, like the wind was blowing in his face.

That kid Harrison also checked in with Dev. His face was all red like he'd been crying. He put the sticker on his shirt and looked back at his parents.

Next up was a very tall kid who looked too big to be going into fifth grade.

"Brandon?" Dev asked, holding out a sticker to the tall kid.

15

"Everyone calls me Weatherman," he said.

"Really? Okay," said Dev, whipping out another name tag and writing "Weatherman."

I started thinking I needed a cool nickname. I was just "Noah." That wasn't cool. Even in fourth grade, people were saying, "Hey, Noah, where's your ark? Haha, haha!" I had to think of something cool before we went to our bunk . . . but what? I could just go by my last name, Benton. That's what Coach calls me at school. And our ninety-year-old English teacher, but he calls me "Mr. Benton." Benton does sound better than Noah. The truth is, I actually like my name . . . I just don't like hearing cracks about it.

The last kid to come up to Dev was short and round with curly brown hair and a red-and-white striped short-sleeved shirt. His parents were also short and round, but adult size.

"Hi, welcome," said Dev. He held out the name tag for him, but he just looked at it and then back at his parents, who shrugged.

"Oh, thank you," he said, taking the sticker. He read it: "Hello, My name is 'Mikey.'" Then he looked up at Dev, excited. "My name's Mikey, too! That's so crazy!"

"No, my name's Dev. That's for you. To put on," said Dev, pointing to Mikey.

Mikey looked back at his parents, who shrugged again.

My parents were still standing there, along with everyone else's parents, with these droopy, sad faces like we were moving away to another continent. Harrison glared at his parents and crossed his arms. It seemed to be the thing to do.

"Can I have everyone's attention?" Dev said, holding up his clipboard. "This is the part where everybody hugs and says, 'goodbye.' I have to take the River Otters to their bunk. I guess any parents who want a tour of the camp should go to the office and talk to Wendy. But tradition is that everyone says 'goodbye' in the parking lot. All the campers will have a chance to call home at the end of the week . . ." Dev flipped through the pages on his clipboard. "Oh, and if anyone still has a cell phone or other electronic devices, they should give them to their parents now."

I looked around to see if anyone was holding out.

"I wish," said Mikey, too loudly. I guess he wished he had a cell phone or something.

Chip's mother took her cell phone out to call someone. After a few seconds, the sound of sea lions barking was coming from somewhere on Chip. He looked all around as if he didn't know where the sound was coming from.

His mother put her hand out, waiting.

Chip slipped the phone out of his back pocket and gave it to her. "I don't know what the big deal is.

17

What kind of camp is this, anyway? What's so wrong with having a cell phone?"

"I don't know, honey, but those are the rules," she said.

I didn't have a cell phone at all, not even at home. My parents weren't cool that way.

Chip's mother put the phone in her bag and opened her arms for a hug. "This is a great camp. So great," she said.

"If you love it so much, why don't you go here and I'll stay at home?" Chip said.

I was starting to wonder if there were any kids who actually wanted to go to this stupid camp. That's when I noticed Weatherman hugging his little brother, who didn't seem to want to let go of him.

Then Weatherman's mother took a picture of the two boys and said, "Maybe you can go here next year." And the little brother started jumping up and down like that was the greatest idea ever.

My mom hugged me. "It's just for three weeks," she said. She looked like she was trying not to cry.

"But they said you could stay for longer if you really like it," said Dad. "And I predict that you will really like it." Then he gave me a big hug.

I shrugged. And the next thing I knew, my parents were getting back into the car and driving away, along with all the other parents, their cars lining up, single file, and disappearing down the dirt road into the pine trees.

We went in the opposite direction. Dev loaded all our bags and stuff onto a wagon and told us to follow him. My stomach felt like it was curling up. I don't know why. I tried to ignore it. *Look at all the trees! Look at all the flowers and grass! Is that a lake over there?* It wasn't working.

Down a long trail were a few wood cabins. Dev stopped at the cabin with the hand-painted sign that said, "River Otters."

When he opened the door, it creaked like a haunted house. "This is it," he said. "Home sweet home."

We dragged our bags inside. There were three bunk beds, six beds in all.

"You guys get to pick out which bed you want," said Dev.

I'd never been in a bunkbed before. I thought it would be kind of fun to be in the top bunk, kind of like sleeping in a treehouse. I heaved my sleeping bag up top. Mikey was already lying across a bottom bunk. Harrison was standing in the middle of the room, holding all his stuff, and looking around in confusion.

Chip and Weatherman also took top bunks.

"That's not fair," said Harrison. "What if I wanted a top bunk?"

"Do you?" Chip asked.

"No, but what if I did?" He carefully placed his sleeping bag and pillow onto a bottom bunk. Then sat down and stared at the remaining empty bed.

Dev had gone to his cabin next door. He returned with a clipboard, looked around the room, and checked some things off his list. "Are you okay?"

Harrison jumped up, snapping out of a trance. "Why is there an empty bed? Is there supposed to be somebody else here?"

Dev looked baffled himself. "Hmmm . . . I don't know. You're right. That's weird."

I couldn't believe what I was hearing. Shouldn't the counselor know where everybody is?

"Okay, roll call," said Dev, flipping the papers on his clipboard. "Okay, Harrison, check. Brandon, aka Weatherman, check. Mikey, check . . ." He looked around. "Oh, Noah—"

"I also have an aka," I said. "What does 'aka' mean again?"

"Also known as," said Dev.

"Yeah, that. My aka is, um, Bent."

"Bent?"

"I mean Bent-ley."

"Bentley?"

"Like the car, Bentley."

"Bentley. Like the car." Dev wrote this down on

his clipboard. "Okay. And Chip, check. So we're good. We're all here."

"But that's only five, and there's six beds," said Harrison.

Dev stared at the empty bed for a moment, then flipped through more pages on his clipboard. "Okay, so, everybody's here, so we can get the show on the road."

"We're doing a show? Already?" Mikey asked, sitting up.

"It's an expression. I mean, we can go do our first activity."

"Oh," said Mikey.

As we followed Dev back through the woods, Chip came up to me and whispered, "Do you think he knows where that other kid is?"

I felt kind of honored that Chip was talking to me. "What kid?"

"The kid that isn't here. Number six."

"You think he knows, and he's not telling?"

"Yeah," said Chip.

&

Dev led us back through the woods to a big stage in the middle of a grassy field. It looked like our stage at school, but without a building around it.

"Whenever we have outdoor assemblies, this is where we gather," Dev said. "It's called the Outdoor Theater."

Chip raised his hand. "Are they going to put on shows here?"

Dev nodded. "Yeah. Maybe your bunk will even put on a show."

"So we *are* doing a show," Mikey whispered loudly.

Kids from all around the camp ran into the field and gathered around the Outdoor Theater. Then the head counselors, Steve and his wife Audrey, waved their hands in the air and blew their whistles. They are old, probably as old as my parents (like forty or fifty years old). Audrey was wearing a hat with plants and twigs stuck to it. Steve was wearing a hat shaped like a canoe.

"Welcome, campers!" Steve shouted. "I know you're excited to be at camp and get things started, so our first order of business is the Get-To-Know-You Scavenger Hunt!" (FYI: Steve shouts everything. He's very excited.)

Steve and Audrey clapped, and everyone clapped along with them. I didn't think a scavenger hunt sounded fun, but maybe it was since everyone was clapping so much.

"Each cabin is a team. Each team gets a list of things to find and collect. The winning cabin gets a special prize," Audrey announced. She said "special prize" like it really was a special prize. So that made me think I really wanted the special prize.

We got our list of things we had to hunt for, plus a big cloth bag. Right away, it did *not* look like this was going to be fun.

Instead of just telling us what we had to hunt for ("find a leaf, find a bottle cap," the usual scavenger hunt stuff), there was a riddle for each thing, and we had to guess what the thing was that we were looking for before we could find it.

"Oh, no," said Chip, after seeing all the words on the paper. "I get the feeling this is secretly a summer school, and they're trying to trick us into learning."

My mouth fell open. I couldn't believe he had the same thought as me! That made me think I was right.

We all read through the riddles. There were five riddles, five things we needed to find.

"Hey, Dev," said Harrison. "Can't you just tell us the answers? Then we don't have to waste all our time trying to solve the riddles."

Dev stood over our group, his arms crossed. "What would be the fun in that?"

Harrison looked at the rest of us and shrugged.

"Read it out loud," Dev advised. "I think that will help."

I took the list and cleared my throat.

"Number one: '*It doesn't make a sound. It doesn't bite. It isn't soft. It's brown, gray, or white. It's not like a sword, but like a shield. You can pick it up when off it has peeled.*'"

"A rock!" Mikey burst out. He clapped his hands together like he was cheering for himself.

I squinted. "Rocks don't peel."

"Oh. Right," said Mikey, dropping his head.

"That was a good guess," Dev said.

Mikey lifted his head. "Yeah?"

"What about a snake? Snakes peel," said Chip.

"You mean, like, not the snake, but the dead skin that comes off the snake," I said.

Chip nodded, and we all looked at Dev, hoping he would tell us if we were on the right track.

Dev smiled and pretended to close the imaginary zipper on his mouth.

Mikey clapped his hands. "Yeah, a snakeskin!"

"But," said Chip, "now that I think of it, snake skins are soft, and it says 'it isn't soft.'"

"I say we go into the woods and look around," said Weatherman.

"I'm hot," said Harrison. "I want to go swimming."

"We can go swimming after," said Dev. "I think that's a good idea to go in the woods and look around."

Other teams were still huddled up, trying to solve all the riddles. As soon as they saw us going into the woods, they followed us.

"That's cheating!" Chip yelled.

"Maybe they already solved the riddles," said Dev. He took a sharp right turn and led our group away from everyone else.

We found a small, open space between the trees, where no one else was around. Chip read the first riddle out loud again.

I leaned my hand on the side of a huge pine tree. It almost got stuck there because of the pine pitch. "Gross!"

"Oh, I wanna see," Mikey said. He put his hand onto the pitch and pulled it away. "Woah, it's like glue."

"Awesome," said Weatherman, who also had to have a try at getting his hand stuck to the tree.

Chip shook his head. "Weirdos."

"Oh, cool, look at this!" I picked up a big piece of bark. The underside was covered with what looked like squiggly carving. "It's like hieroglyphics." I held it out for all the guys to see.

"Whaaaat . . . ?" Chip grabbed it from me. He studied it. "It's like a secret language or something."

Dev leaned over the group to see the bark. "That looks like an insect was eating it."

"Where's the bag?" I asked. "Let's save it. Maybe we can get extra points."

"Yeah, put it in the bag," said Mikey.

Weatherman had taken the job of carrying the bag. He opened it up, and I put the bark in, very carefully.

"You guys, should we do the next riddle?" I asked.

"This is taking forever," said Harrison.

We all looked at each other and shrugged.

Chip handed the list back to me. "You read it."

"Okay . . . number two," I read, "'It *always starts off small, and depending on where it falls, it could be the shortest or the tallest one of all.*'"

"That's easy. It's a seed," said Chip.

"Yeah, that's what I think," I said.

"Yeah, that's what I think, too," said Mikey.

We all looked up at Dev.

He nodded.

I looked at the paper. "Okay, number three . . ."

"But don't we have to find a seed?" Mikey asked in a panic.

We started searching around on the ground.

Weatherman went the farthest away and picked up something. "An acorn's a seed, right?" he asked.

"Yup," said Dev.

"Okay, number three," I began again.

"*Some are quite poisonous, some are quite good. Some live in the grass; some live on wood. Some are pretty, some are plain; all have a cover for when it rains. Just answer the riddle, and don't try to touch because the wrong kind can hurt you so much.*"

"Poison dart frog!" Mikey yelled.

"If it's a poison dart frog, then some of them can't be good," I said.

"Oh."

"Spiders could be poisonous or not poisonous," said Chip.

"Yeah, it's a spider!" Mikey yelled.

"How are we supposed to catch a spider?" asked Harrison.

"You're not," said Dev, pulling a pen out of his shirt pocket. "You have to write down your answer."

I was going to write "spider" on the paper, but then I stopped. "Is that the right answer, Dev? Spider?"

Dev shrugged and looked around at the sky.

I glanced at the other guys. "I'll put spider, but we can change it."

"This is so boring," Harrison whined. "I want to go back to the cabin."

"Maybe you should read the next riddle," Dev said.

I handed the sheet to Harrison.

He looked at it for a second, then handed it back to me. "It's too boring."

"I'll read it," said Chip, grabbing the sheet.

"Number four: '*It doesn't eat. It doesn't pee—*'"

"Ewwww!" everyone squealed.

Chip laughed. "'*It can smell, but it can't see. It has a tongue, but it can't talk; it helps you move around the block.*'"

"How are we supposed to put a car in the bag?" asked Weatherman.

"Yeah, cars are heavy," said Mikey.

Chip and Harrison looked at Weatherman, impressed.

I wasn't so sure. "Cars eat gas."

Chip looked at me like I was crazy. "Cars can't eat."

"Also," I said, "cars don't have tongues."

"Oh," said Chip.

We were all stumped. I took my yo-yo out of my pocket and started spinning it. The other guys sat down in a circle on the pine needles and looked up at Dev.

"Cool yo-yo," said Chip.

It was cool. It was my lucky yo-yo.

"Give us a clue, Dev. Please," I said.

Everyone begged, "Please, please, Dev!"

"Well," he said, "A car is a good guess because it doesn't have to be something in nature."

We all looked at each other. That was a good clue.

"A horse!" Mikey yelled.

"Horses have to eat," said Chip. "And pee."

"Oh. Yeah."

"Good guess, Mikey," said Dev. "Horses have tongues, and they help you get around."

I took the sheet from Chip and read the riddle to myself. "What isn't alive, but it has a tongue?"

"These questions aren't fair. They're too hard," Harrison moaned.

"But you guys are doing such a good job," said Dev.

We were doing a bad job. These riddles were too hard.

"Do we have to solve all the riddles?" Harrison asked.

"No," said Dev. "But then you won't win the prize."

I really wanted to win the prize. It was a "special prize."

"How many more questions are there?" asked Harrison.

"Yeah, how many?" asked Mikey.

"Just one more," I said, checking the paper.

"Read it," said Chip.

"Number five: 'It is small and light and thin. It can end a story, and it can begin.' That's it."

"They're crazy!" Harrison burst out. "Do they think we're in high school or something?"

"Yeah, these riddles are for people in college," said Mikey.

"I think you can do it," said Dev.

I shook my head. "It's too hard." I read riddle number three again. "Dev, can I have your pen back?" I reached out for the pen but didn't get hold of it, and it fell into the pine needles. When I picked it up, a bunch of pine needles came with it. Then the pine needles stuck to my hand because my hand still had pitch on it. So I tried to wipe the pine needles off on my shorts, and then I had pine needles stuck to my shorts.

"Can we just guess?" said Chip.

"I don't think number three is 'spiders,'" I said.

"Yeah, me neither," said Mikey.

"Spiders don't have covers from the rain," I said.

"Where are they supposed to go when it rains?" asked Mikey.

"I don't know," I said.

Dev looked at his watch. "Let's walk back to the outdoor theater, and maybe you'll find the answers on the way."

We followed Dev through the forest, walking a different way back. We went around some boulders and dead trees lying on the ground.

"Why do they call you 'Weatherman'?" I asked as we were climbing over a mound of rocks.

Weatherman stopped and looked up. Then he sniffed the air and looked at the sky again. "We're not going swimming after this. I can tell you that."

I looked up at the blue sky. "Why not?"

"Hey, look! A chipmunk!" Weatherman said.

A chipmunk was standing on top of a log. When he saw us, he jumped inside the log. We all ran over to see if we could find him, but it was dark inside, so we couldn't see anything.

"What are these?" asked Dev, pointing to bright orange mushrooms growing on the side of the log.

"Mushrooms," I said.

"Right. Mushrooms," Dev repeated.

Chip and I looked at each other and said at the same time: "Mushrooms!"

"No, duh," said Harrison.

"I don't get it," said Mikey.

I read the third question again: "'*Some are quite poisonous, some are quite good. Some live in the grass; some live on wood. Some are pretty, some are plain; all have a cover for when it rains. Just answer the riddle, and don't try to touch, because the wrong kind can hurt you so much.*'"

I crossed out the word "spider" and wrote "mushrooms."

Everyone looked at the paper.

"Can't we keep both answers in case 'spider' is right?" asked Mikey.

Dev shook his head. "I think you have to pick one. Get it? Pick one? Ha ha ha ha! Like, pick a mushroom, only, don't pick a mushroom because it might be poisonous." Dev continued laughing at his own joke.

"I don't get it," said Mikey. "Does that mean 'mushroom' isn't the right answer?"

"He was making a joke. About picking mushrooms," I said.

"But he said not to pick mushrooms! Because mushrooms is wrong!" Mikey looked so confused; I thought his head was going to explode.

"Mushrooms is right," I said.

"But, but, but—" Mikey said.

"You guys, look!" Chip screamed, pointing to the opening outside the forest.

We could see another group making their way to the Outdoor Theater.

"Oh, no!" I yelled and started running out of the forest, with the rest of the guys trailing after me. I couldn't bear the thought of seeing another bunk win the special prize.

When we reached the Outdoor Theater, the other team was asking Camp Director Steve a question, not handing in their bag and sheet of riddles.

"We still have a chance!" I said, reading the riddles again. "'*It doesn't eat. It doesn't pee. It can smell, but it can't see. It has a tongue, but it can't talk. It helps you move around the block.*'"

"A dog?" Mikey said, flopping down on the grass

and pulling off his sneaker. He turned it upside down and shook it until a piece of bark fell out.

"It can't be an animal because it doesn't eat, remember?" I was starting to feel sorry for Mikey because he was trying so hard to solve the riddles, but none of his guesses were right. Then, as he was pulling his shoe back on, something came to me. "Hey, Mikey, what's that thing called underneath where your shoelaces are?"

Mikey looked from his sneaker to me. "I don't know, but it's really annoying."

"The tongue!" Chip and Weatherman burst out at the same time.

"It helps you get around the block!" I said.

"That's the answer?" Mikey asked. Then he shrugged and pulled his sneaker back off, tossing it into the bag.

"You could just write down 'shoe,'" said Dev.

But Mikey shook his head. "We have to win."

A bunk called the Gray Wolves was watching us. They saw Mikey put his shoe into the bag. So then a few of them took their shoes off and threw them into their bag.

"Oh, no!" Chip screamed.

Then it got even worse because Steve picked up his bullhorn to make an announcement. "Attention campers! You have one minute to turn in your answers. Whoever has the most correct answers wins the prize!"

"It's not fair. They made it too hard," Harrison whined.

We gathered around the riddles sheet. I checked off the ones we had answered. It was horrible. We only had three out of five solved. "What can end a story?" I asked, clicking the pen nervously.

"A book?" said Chip.

"A movie?" said Weatherman.

"But it has to be small and light and thin," I said.

"A really easy book," said Chip.

"Thirty seconds!" Steve yelled through his bullhorn.

Other groups were running toward Steve from all directions.

CHAPTER 3
THE GRAY WOLVES

"Oh no, you guys!"

I started to write down "book" for the answer to number five, but I dropped the pen again. As I picked it up, it came to me! The *pen* was "small and light and thin.'" I wrote down the word "pen," took the bag from Weatherman and ran top speed over to Steve. I handed him the bag and the paper at the same time as three other teams came charging up, holding their bags out.

Steve took the bag and paper from me. He looked over the answers on the paper, then opened up the bag to check what was inside.

The rest of the River Otters caught up to me. Chip was grumbling that we didn't have the answer to number one.

"Maybe he won't notice," Weatherman whispered.

"If nobody else gets them all right, we could still win," I said.

After a really, really long time, Steve looked up from our bag, smiling. "We have a winner!" he yelled through his bullhorn.

All the other teams let out a disappointed "Aww!"

We all looked at each other and then to Steve, totally confused. "Whaaaat?"

A team called The Mallard Ducks skidded to a stop in front of Steve, but they were a second too late. They looked angry. "Can you tell us the answers?"

"Yeah, tell us the answers!" the other groups were shouting.

"That's what I was just about to do!" Steve declared, his bullhorn just inches from our faces.

The whole rest of the camp gathered around to hear the answers to the riddles. Meanwhile, Chip, Harrison, Mikey, Weatherman, and I were looking at each other in a panic.

"But I thought we didn't get all the answers," Mikey said too loudly.

Dev just stood there, half-smiling, not worried at all.

But a bunk called the Gray Wolves were giving us the evil eye. They must have heard Mikey, and now they were mad.

"Okay," Steve began, "number one: 'It doesn't make a sound; it doesn't bite; it isn't soft; it's brown, gray, or white. It's not like a sword, but like a shield; you can pick it up when off it has peeled.'"

Oh no, oh no, oh no. That's the one we didn't get.

He reached into the bag and held up the piece of bark we thought we could use for extra credit.

I felt faint and sweaty. Didn't he see what that was? That was cool insect hieroglyphics. It wasn't the answer. "Um, but . . ." I heard myself mumbling.

"Bark!" said Steve. "Raise your hand if you got number one."

We looked around. Most of the teams were raising their hands. We couldn't believe it. We got the answer by accident.

"Good job, everybody!"

Mikey started clapping. Then he stopped. "Wait. How did we do that?"

The Wolves were still glaring at us.

We looked at Dev. He smiled and gave us the thumbs up.

Steve went through the rest of the answers. No other group got all the answers correct. One group had put a snail in their bag as the answer to number three. Steve told them to go carefully and put it back where they found it.

"Congratulations to the River Otters!" Steve yelled. "You win the official prize—chocolate cupcakes with fudge frosting!"

We all jumped around wildly, screaming and cheering for our cupcakes. Cupcakes sounded really good right now. Lunch had been so long ago.

Just then, Steve's wife Audrey took the bullhorn. "Okay, campers. Please go back to your cabins to get changed for swimming. See you at Mudd Lake!"

Mud Lake? What kind of camp was this? Did they really expect us to splash around in mud? How were we supposed to swim and play Marco Polo? Gross.

"I don't want to go swimming in mud," Harrison said, as we were walking back to our cabin.

"It's named after a guy with the last name Mudd," said Dev. "It's not a lake made out of mud."

"Oh, okay," said Harrison.

"When are we having our cupcakes?" Mikey asked.

"Yeah, what about the cupcakes?" I asked.

"The cupcakes are for dessert, after supper," said Dev.

Just thinking about the cupcakes made me even hungrier. Why couldn't we have the cupcakes now?

When I opened the door to the cabin, a super-strong stench hit me in the face.

"It smells like pickles in here!" I yelled.

"Uh-oh," said Mikey, running to his duffle bag. He

pulled out a big jar of pickles. It was dripping with pickle juice. "I don't know how this jar got opened."

"When you opened it," said Chip. He looked over Mikey's bag of clothes. "Now you're going to smell like pickles . . . forever."

Mikey shrugged, took a pickle out of the jar, and chomped into it.

That's when I noticed my yo-yo wasn't in my pocket. I was wearing shorts that had a lot of pockets. I checked every pocket, but it wasn't there! I looked all over the cabin, but I couldn't find it.

"What are you looking for?" asked Chip.

"My yo-yo." I lifted up everybody's sleeping bags and even checked under their mattresses. I ran back outside the door and looked around.

The other guys came outside to help me look.

"It could be anywhere," said Chip.

"You had it on the Scavenger Hunt," said Weatherman.

"Did you check your pockets?" asked Mikey.

"Yeah, I checked my pockets," I said.

Mikey stuffed his hand into his pocket and pulled out something. "Wow, awesome." He held up a box of gum. "Look what I found!"

Everyone stuck out a hand to get some. Mikey gave each of us a single, tiny piece of gum and then poured the rest of the box into his mouth.

We all checked our pockets for candy. Harrison pulled out a package of tissues. Chip had a superball. Weatherman had a fortune from a fortune cookie.

"What's it say?" I asked.

Weatherman opened the tiny piece of paper. "Beware of dark skies. Lucky numbers: 8, 50, 11, 7, 15, 61."

"Wow," said Mikey. "You've got a lot of lucky numbers."

"What does 'beware of dark skies' mean?" I asked, checking my pockets again.

Weatherman shrugged.

CHAPTER 4
MYSTERY IN THE DINING HALL

Everyone got changed into their swim trunks and met Dev outside the cabin. Everyone except Weatherman, that is.

"Aren't you going swimming?" Dev asked.

Weatherman had on a rain poncho. "Nobody's going swimming," he said.

"What does that even mean?" asked Mikey.

I wanted to go swimming, but I really needed my yo-yo. "Dev, I can't find my yo-yo," I said.

"It's probably in Lost and Found," he said. "We can check after swimming."

We marched along a narrow dirt path, winding through the trees from our cabin down to the lake.

From the looks of it, the water was a dark blue-green and not the muddy brown mudhole I was expecting. But the mud was probably going to get churned up once we all got into the water and started kicking and splashing around.

There were lifeguard chairs set up along the shore, and there were ropes attached to buoys dividing the water into different sections.

We were one of the first bunks to reach the water, but then one by one, other groups started to appear. That's when the Gray Wolves came up to us. There were six of them. The tallest and biggest one was named Justin.

"We know you cheated," he said.

We all looked at each other, confused.

"Yeah, we heard you say you didn't have all the answers," said the smallest guy. He had wild hair and bright red sneakers. They called him Crazy Alex. He acted like the leader.

"We didn't cheat," said Chip.

Dev suddenly popped up in the middle of everybody. "Let's go swimming, guys."

Our whole bunk ran away from the Gray Wolves as fast as we could. But the second our feet touched the lake, we heard the boom of thunder, followed by every single counselor blowing their whistles and shouting: "Out of the water!" Storm clouds suddenly blew across the lake and started pouring rain.

"Told ya we weren't swimming," Weatherman said, putting the hood up on his rain poncho.

"How'd you know it was going to rain?" Mikey asked.

Weatherman shrugged. "I don't know. I just know."

"Cool."

"Everybody, go to the dining hall!" Steve shouted with his bullhorn.

Everyone started running up the hill.

But I saw something weird in the water. It was dark and looked like a big snake head bobbing up and down.

"Look!" I pointed to the strange creature bobbing in the water, but nobody was around. I watched a little longer, hoping to see whatever it was again, but then Dev called me to catch up with the rest of the bunk.

It took forever for the entire camp to get into the dining hall, and then we had to wait for Steve and Audrey to get there. The Gray Wolves sat at a table next to ours and gave us the evil eye.

I remembered my yo-yo was still missing. "Dev, can we go to Lost and Found?"

Just then, Steve yelled, "Time to sing the camp song!"

Audrey jumped up and down. "And time to learn the camp song if you are a new camper!"

I didn't want to sing. I just wanted to find my yo-yo.

"We can go after," Dev said.

Steve grabbed a guitar, and then Audrey also got a guitar. And then a bunch of the counselors ran into the center of the room where Steve and Audrey were clapping and swaying.

Audrey started singing, and then Steve sort of joined in, but didn't seem to know the words.

"*Welcome to Summer Camp Academy, where we have lots of fun! Swimming and hiking, learning and growing, and singing songs! Making memories that last a lifetime! Summer Camp Aca-de-my!*"

If my friends from my town were here, we would be looking at each other right now, and Josh would be saying that Steve and Audrey just made that song up. It didn't sound like a real song, and the other counselors were just clapping along; they weren't singing. I wish Josh was here.

Then the weirdest thing happened: Chip leaned over and said, "They just made that up."

I couldn't believe it. "Yeah! That's what I think!"

"Okay, campers," Steve said, waving a hand in the air. "Listen up, your fantastic gourmet meal isn't quite ready yet, so that means we have plenty of time for more songs!"

"Yay!" Audrey yelled. She jumped up so fast she banged herself in the head with her guitar.

Mikey was holding his stomach. "But I'm really

hungry."

"It's time for some folk songs from long ago," said Audrey, strumming her guitar.

As soon as Audrey opened her mouth to sing, a man in a big white apron stepped out of the kitchen and blew a whistle.

"Supper's ready!" he said. He had a long gray ponytail and tie-dyed t-shirt on.

Audrey looked sad that she couldn't sing her song.

All the campers popped out of their seats and ran top speed to the food line.

"Single file!" Steve yelled in his bullhorn.

Nobody was listening.

Kids were grabbing trays and holding them out for the cook and the counselors who were serving the food.

"What is it?" Harrison asked.

"I don't know, and I don't care, as long as it's not vegetables," said Mikey, getting a heaping plate of stuff on top of other stuff.

Whatever it was, it looked pretty good. It would have been better if it was a hotdog or a hamburger, but at least it wasn't fish.

"Everyone, please thank our Master Chef, Bob Barley, for preparing such a nutritious and delicious meal!" Audrey yelled.

"Thank you," everyone mumbled.

I sat down and shoveled a pile of food into my mouth. It was bad. In fact, it was pretty terrible. The chunks of chicken were kind of squishy, and I don't even know what the other stuff was.

Mikey looked like he was going to cry. "Dev, what is this stuff?"

Dev was happily eating it. "It's chicken a la king on mashed potatoes. Only, it's not chicken, it's tofu, and it's not just potatoes, it's potatoes and cauliflower."

Mikey, who had already picked all the carrots and celery out of the sauce, pushed his plate away in horror. "It's all vegetables!" he screamed. "There's NO FOOD!"

Everyone at the table looked as horrified as Mikey that they weren't eating real food.

"It's definitely gross, but I'm really hungry," I said.

"What's tofu, anyway?" Mikey cried. "Isn't that like a sea sponge or mold or something?"

"No," said Chip. "It's algae mixed with eggs."

"Gross!" everyone screamed.

Dev held up a piece of tofu. "Guys, come on. It's made from soybeans. No worries."

"Soy Beans? That's another VEGETABLE," Mikey said. He shook his head in disgust.

Dev nodded. "I see your dilemma. But what are you going to eat then?"

"Can I have a sandwich?"

46

"Let me check." Dev disappeared into the kitchen.

"That's not fair," said Harrison. "I want a sandwich."

I held up a forkful of the white stuff. "The potato part has potato in it," I said.

"Potato's a vegetable," said Weatherman.

Mikey looked worried.

"Yeah . . . what do you think they make French fries out of . . . usually?" I offered.

"If you close your eyes, it's not that bad," said Chip.

Just then, Dev returned with a peanut butter and jelly sandwich. He was about to hand it to Mikey, but then yanked it away. "Oh, wait, can you eat peanut butter?"

"Of course, I can eat peanut butter," said Mikey. "But . . . Can I have baloney instead?"

Dev shook his head slowly. "Sorry, bud, I don't think they have any baloney."

Audrey was holding up a tray of chocolate cupcakes.

"Look! Look!" I said.

Steve raised his bullhorn. "Attention, everyone! It's time to present the prize to the winners of the Scavenger Hunt. Come on up here, River Otters!"

We ran to get our cupcakes, nearly knocking Audrey over.

"Can I have two?" asked Mikey.

"We need to make sure everyone gets one," said Audrey.

"Attention! Your counselors will be coming around with beautiful sliced watermelon and apple cobbler! A special treat for the first night of camp!" Steve barked.

Mikey stuffed half the cupcake into his mouth, and then scrunched up his face in disgust. He looked at the cupcake. "There's little green things in it. What is this?"

"Oh, that's zucchini," said Audrey.

Mikey's eyes bulged out. "I'm allergic to vegetables!"

Audrey laughed. "No, you're not! Your mother said you'd say that." She pointed proudly at the cupcake. "It tastes good, doesn't it?"

"No," said Mikey, but then he turned away from Audrey and stuffed the rest of the cupcake into his mouth.

A couple of the Gray Wolves, Justin, and Crazy Alex (his parents probably didn't give him that name) came over to our table.

"How do those cheater cupcakes taste, cheaters?" Justin asked.

"Like the greatest cupcakes in the entire world," Chip said.

"Really? Audrey put broccoli or something in

them last year," said Crazy Alex.

"Not this time! They're awesome," said Chip.

Mikey opened his mouth, but Chip gave him a little kick.

"Why are you calling us cheaters?" I asked. "We didn't cheat."

"You didn't find all the stuff on the scavenger hunt fair and square," said Justin.

"We still found it," I said. (Probably not loud enough for them to hear me.)

"River Otters!" Steve blasted through his bullhorn. "You get to pick the next contest!"

Two counselors carried a giant cardboard wheel into the center of the room.

"We need a volunteer from the River Otters to spin the wheel!"

We all raised our hands.

Steve pointed to me. "I saw your hand first. Come on up and give it a great, big spin!"

CHAPTER 5
SPIN THE WHEEL

I ran up and spun it as hard as I could.

Everyone was clapping and shouting out: "Come on, Bake-off!" "Come on, Play-off!" "Quiz Bowl! Quiz Bowl!"

The wheel slowed down just before "Academic Quiz Bowl" and then clicked over to "Navigation-off."

A lot of people clapped. I didn't know what "Navigation-off" meant, but maybe it was a good thing. I was definitely glad it didn't land on "Academic Quiz Bowl." That sounded about as good as "Spelling Bee."

Steve and Audrey applauded. "Well done!"

The whole bunk looked confused. But the Gray Wolves were staring daggers at us.

"Nice play, Einstein," Justin snapped as I went past him on the way back to my seat.

"Wow, this is a big one, you guys! Really big!" Steve boomed. "For the Navigation-off, we'll give you a map, and some other supplies, and your prize will be waiting at your destination point."

Mikey glared at his plate of food. "If it's a bag of carrots, I don't want to find it."

Audrey pointed to the wheel. "Whoever finds their prize first, gets to pick the next activity."

"If we have to spin the wheel, then we aren't really picking the activity," Harrison said.

"We need to know what the prize is, so we know if we want to find it," said Mikey.

"It's marshmallows," Audrey whispered loudly.

Mikey clapped. "Finally, real food."

Audrey and Steve got their guitars back out and split the room into two groups. We sang "Row Row Row Your Boat" in a round, and then the "Going on a Bear Hunt" song.

By the time we got out of the dining hall, it was dark outside.

"What about Lost and Found?" I asked.

"Oh yeah," said Dev.

We went to the main office. There was a sign with a basket that said "Lost & Found" in the corner of the room. The basket was already filled up with hats, and sweatshirts, and flipflops, and sunglasses, and even a flashlight keychain. But my yo-yo wasn't there.

"I have to find it," I said.

"It'll show up," said Dev.

We had to walk through the dark woods to get to our cabin. The more we walked, the darker it got. Everyone stopped talking. We heard an owl calling, "Hoo hoo hoo hoo . . ."

Mikey grabbed Dev's arm. "It's a werewolf!"

"No, Mikey, that's a great horned owl."

"A great horned owl? Do they eat people?"

Chip let out a laugh. "Owls are birds. How's it going to eat a person?"

"He said it's a *great horned* owl! He could probably stab your head off with his horns!"

"Owls just eat rodents, I think."

"He thinks," Mikey whispered.

It got quiet again, as we were almost at our cabins. There were no lights on. The trees were blocking out the moon. Dev had a flashlight, but it wasn't working. He kept shaking it.

I could hardly see the pathway. The deeper we walked into the woods, the darker it got.

"BOO!" screamed Crazy Alex, jumping out from behind a tree.

We screamed our heads off.

The rest of the Gray Wolves came out from behind the trees. They were laughing at us.

Justin gave Crazy Alex a high-five. "Ha, ha! Busted!"

Dev shined his flashlight on Justin's face. "Where's your counselor?"

"We don't know."

Justin and Crazy Alex looked at each other and snickered.

"That's not cool," said Dev. "I'm serious."

"Uh—he went back to the cabin already because Ryan had to go to the bathroom."

"Then you guys should come with us. We'll drop you off."

The Gray Wolves had their cabin not far from ours. They were pretty quiet on the walk to their grove, up until they got there. Then Crazy Alex pointed up into the treetops.

"Don't forget, the Zombie Crow lives in the trees."

We looked up at the black tree branches above our heads.

"Don't look up! That's what he wants you to do!"

I looked away quickly. "What's the Zombie Crow?"

Dev shook his head.

"Are you kidding? What do you think happened to the Lost Camper?" asked Crazy Alex.

Weatherman darted his eyes up, nervously. "What's the Lost Camper?"

Dev was still shaking his head. "No, no . . ."

Justin smiled. "A long time ago, back in the 1980s, there was a kid at this camp, it was called

54

something different back then, and he went out into the Mysterious Woods on a scavenger hunt or something, and he got lost, and the last time they saw him was just before the Zombie Crow swooped down and grabbed him and flew away—"

"Will you guys knock it off?" Dev interrupted. "Just go in your cabin, okay?"

Mikey glanced sideways at Dev. "I thought birds couldn't kill people."

Crazy Alex covered his mouth to squelch a laugh. "Just watch out tomorrow."

"What do you mean?" I asked.

"The Navigation-off, duh. Your map could lead you right into the Mysterious Woods. And then, who knows." Crazy Alex shrugged his shoulders like it was already a done deal that our bunk would disappear FOREVER.

Dev let out a loud sigh and waved his flashlight, directing the Gray Wolves to go to their cabin.

Back at our cabin, it was pitch dark except for the battery-powered lanterns and our flashlights. Dev told us to turn off the lanterns and go to sleep. It was windy outside, so the cabin was making creaking sounds.

I kept my flashlight on to write a letter to my parents.

Dear Mom and Dad:

You said I could call you and you would take me home at the end of the week if I didn't like camp. So far, I don't like it so much. Some things are good, some things are bad. A bad thing is I lost my lucky yo-yo. It's the red one. They won't let me call you or email you, so I am writing this letter, but doesn't it take a month for a letter to get to you?

My bunkmates are Chip (he is funny, and we would be friends if he was at my school), Mikey (he is probably here instead of summer school because he has a lot to learn), Weatherman (he knew it was going to start raining today even when it didn't look like it!), and Harrison (he doesn't act like he likes camp, but he didn't say he wants to go home).

We are called the River Otters. This isn't a cool name. There is another bunk called the Gray Wolves. They have a cool name, but they are mean. Maybe if they were called the Gray Squirrels, they would be nicer.

We won the scavenger hunt today. That means we got cupcakes for a prize. There was zucchini in the cupcakes! That was gross. We also got to pick the next contest. We picked the Navigation-off. That means we have to learn how to find our way around.

I think camp is hard, like school, in a way. I thought camp was supposed to be fun. What if we get lost in the woods?

Love,

Noah

I turned off my flashlight. Now it was really, really dark. "You guys, do you think the Zombie Crow thing is real?"

Chip sat up in his bunk. "What do you mean 'real'?"

"I mean, what if there's something that jumps out of the trees?"

"It's real. I've heard about it," said Harrison.

Mikey sat up. "I knew it! I knew it!"

"*Shhh*. Go to sleep," Weatherman said. "Those guys are just trying to scare us."

The wind continued to blow. Even the trees were making creaking sounds.

Just then, BAM! Something landed with a thud on the roof of the cabin. We all screamed.

CHAPTER 6
THE ZOMBIE CROW

"It's the Zombie Crow!"

Harrison pulled his sleeping bag over his head. "Somebody go check!"

"I'm not going out there," said Mikey.

"Me neither!"

"Not me!"

"Somebody go get Dev," said Chip.

"That would mean going outside!" I said.

Everyone was quiet, listening for more sounds of the Zombie Crow. It didn't help that the wind was blowing stronger, and the forest was creaking and howling.

Then, just when Harrison uncovered his head, we heard a terrible scraping sound on the roof.

"He's coming!" Mikey screamed.

We were all screaming and screaming at the top of our lungs. The screaming went on forever.

Suddenly, the door swung open! All we could do was hide under our covers and scream our heads off. "Aaaaaaaaaaaaaaah!"

Then we heard a voice over our chorus of screams.

"Stop screaming, you guys! You're going to wake up the whole camp."

I lowered my covers just enough to see who was standing in the doorway. "It's Dev."

All the guys looked out from their sleeping bags and blankets.

Dev picked up the lantern by the door and turned it on. "Why are you screaming?"

I was screaming so hard I could hardly breathe. "We thought you were the Zombie Crow."

"He's still out there!" Harrison shrieked.

Dev shook his head. "I didn't see anything out there."

"We heard it on the roof," I panted.

That's when the scraping sound happened again, and something black fell down outside the window.

"Aaaaaaaaaaaaaaaaaaaahhhh!" we all screamed.

Even Dev jumped. Then he dared to go outside and look around. We saw him outside the window where the Zombie Crow had fallen. "You guys, it's just a tree branch." Then he came back inside and told us to go to sleep.

But I was afraid to go to sleep. I guess I did, though, eventually.

CHAPTER 7
ORANGE MORNING SILVERSTEIN

I don't know what a "hippie" is, but when Dev was talking to the other counselors at breakfast, they kept saying the Arts and Crafts teacher was a "hippie." As usual, Harrison was reading a book as we walked from the dining hall down a narrow, winding path, deep into the woods, in a direction we had never gone before. The deeper we went, the more mosquitos were surrounding us and flying in our faces.

"Aaaahhh!" Mikey screamed, waving his arms around frantically. "They're attacking me! Can't we go back to the dining hall? I can't take it!"

Dev pulled out a can of bug spray. "Did you put on mosquito repellant today?"

Mikey was slapping his arms and legs and then twirling around to escape the mosquito swarm. "No. I put it on yesterday."

"You gotta put it on every day. It washes off."

"But I didn't take a shower last night."

"Okay, so, you're supposed to take a shower every night."

"Why? We're just gonna get dirty and have to put sunscreen and bug repellent on all over again," said Mikey. He stood still and held his arms out so Dev could spray him all over with the mosquito repellent.

"Mikey's right, for once," said Chip. "Why do you have to wash all that stuff off if you're just going to put it right back on and get all dirty and stuff anyway?"

"If we got to go swimming in the lake every day, we wouldn't have to take a shower," I said. I didn't mind taking showers, but wasn't it practically as good swimming in the lake?

"Yeah," said Mikey, turning around for Dev to spray his back.

"You have to take a shower. That's life," said Dev. "Come on."

We kept walking down the narrow path, with roots and rocks in the way. Harrison stumbled a few times, but I caught him. He said I could read the book he was reading when he was done with it, so I wanted him to get done with it. It was actually a graphic novel and didn't have a lot of words, so it looked pretty good.

Suddenly the path ended, and we were standing in an open area with chunks of bark on the ground and patches of tall grass around a little cabin. It looked like a house in a fairy tale, with colored cellophane butterflies in the windows and little purple flowers growing by the entrance. Dev opened the creaky wooden door and stuck his head in.

"Hi," he said, then waved for us to come in with him.

Inside, the cabin was bright and sunny. There were mobiles of origami birds floating around the room and yarn wrapped around popsicle sticks, making multicolored woven squares.

"Come on in, everyone," the Arts and Crafts teacher said, almost like she was singing. "There's a stool for everyone . . . that's right. Sit wherever you feel comfortable."

The tables were covered with years and years of paint, and glue, and glitter. There were even names carved into the wood, and notes written in permanent marker, like: "Snapping Turtles Rock!" and "1989 4-eva." I wasn't sure what that meant. It was hard to imagine kids being at this camp so long ago. I started to wonder if it had always been called "Summer Camp Academy." There's no way that after the first couple of years, kids wouldn't have caught on and said, "It's summer school! I'm not going!"

I scooched my stool closer to the table so I could find more notes written by kids from summers past. "Beware the Zombie Crow" was written in black with scary eyes in place of the letter "O".

The teacher had very long, straight brown hair and she was wearing a long dress with big sleeves. She waved her arms slowly in the air. "Welcome to the arts and crafts workshop. My name is Orange Morning Silverstein. I'm here to assist you in your creative exploration."

I didn't know what she was talking about, starting with what she said her name was.

"This is a free space for you to express your-selves. If you see something in the room you want to make, I'm here to help you. If you think of something that you'd like to make and would like me to share my thoughts about what kind of supplies might help you bring your dream into reality, that's what I want to do . . . the supplies are—"

She backed up and waved her hand over a bunch of carts with trays filled with all kinds of crazy things. There wasn't just markers and construction paper, but tiny pinecones, paper towel rolls, dried flowers, old magazines, different colors of yarn, bottle caps . . . I could go on all day. This lady had a lot of supplies.

Harrison wasn't looking at any of it; he was trying to finish his book.

Mikey raised his hand. "Mrs. Orange?"

"It's just Orange. Morning. Orange Morning," she corrected. "And you don't have to raise your hand here. You can say, 'I'd like to share' or 'I was wondering.' Do you want to try that?" she asked.

Mikey looked confused. "What? Are you going to make us learn stuff?"

"I'm here to learn from you," she said.

Mikey looked more confused. He scanned the room. "I don't know a lot about art. I probably won't be able to teach you anything."

Orange Morning smiled. "We'll see. I think everyone can teach, and everyone can learn."

I still didn't know what she was talking about, but she did use the word "learn," so it sounded like school was happening. The thing is, I like art, even in school, and Mrs. Orange Morning seemed like she was going to be nice.

"Today is a great day to explore," she said. "There's lots of amazing found objects in here and different colors and textures for you to work with. Please feel free to get up and look inside every bin and shelf and gather together whatever you would like to create and express with."

I had my eye on that bin of tiny pinecones and

jumped up to get them. On a little table nearby, I saw what looked like a big map on yellow paper. There were a candle and matches beside that. The edges of the map were jagged and black like it had been burned. That made it look like an old map from a pirate ship.

"Can I make a pirate map?" I asked.

Orange Morning slipped over to the little table and turned the map over so no one could see it. "Sure, you can."

That's when the cabin started to rumble and shake. Unfortunately, it was the Gray Wolves busting in to ruin everything. They were so loud wherever they went. They were laughing and punching each other, and acting like the arts and crafts cabin was their own place.

Orange Morning looked confused herself. She waited for the Gray Wolves' counselor to come in. He was trailing far behind.

"Hi," Orange Morning said, smiling. She was always smiling. I guess she was always happy.

"Hi," said Brian.

"Um . . . I don't think you're scheduled to be here right now," said Orange.

Brian pulled a folded piece of paper out of his pocket and studied it. "No, it says we are here now. Maybe we're supposed to double up."

"Hmmm . . ." said Orange.

Meanwhile, the Gray Wolves were circling around the room, touching everything, even the stuff everybody from my bunk had already taken out of the bins. Crazy Alex went right over to the tiny table and turned over the map. He looked up to see if Orange was watching, but she was busy looking at Brian's piece of paper, trying to figure out if the Gray Wolves really were supposed to be in Arts and Crafts now.

I had a feeling Crazy Alex wasn't supposed to be looking at the map. It probably had something to do with the Navigation-Off. The next thing I knew, he was waving over Justin, to look at the map with him. I was getting mad because it wasn't fair what they were doing, but I didn't know what to do about it.

"I think this might be a tiny glitch in the scheduling," Orange Morning said to Brian. "I wish we could all be together. I wish the whole camp could fit in this cabin, but, hmmm." She never saw Crazy Alex take his cell phone out of his pocket and take a picture of the map!

I nudged Chip and whispered loudly, "He has a cell phone!" I knew this would make Chip mad since he had to give up his cell phone on the first day of camp.

Chip looked up from the table, where he had been carving his name into the wood with a ballpoint pen. "No way!"

Orange Morning looked up. "Ooooh, sounds like we're in for some creative projects!" She raised her eyebrows at Chip, waiting for him to explain his big art plans.

But Chip just frowned, and leaned his head to the side, like he was trying to point to Crazy Alex.

Orange Morning leaned her head to the side, too. "Are you going to make a sculpture of your head?"

Chip shook his head frantically. Meanwhile, Crazy Alex had put his cell phone back in his pocket, and he and Justin were snickering at Chip.

Orange Morning smiled. "Okay, well, when you're ready to share, we are here to listen." She picked up a stool that was against the wall and stuck it between Chip and me. "I think we can pull up some more stools. Yes, I think we can do it! Let's share this space," she said. "Here, why don't you sit right here," she told Crazy Alex, pointing to the stool between Chip and me.

Crazy Alex made a weird snorting sound and then sat down, crashing into both of us to make more room for himself. He squinted at Chip, but Chip just looked away. Nobody was going to tell on him, and he knew it.

Brian helped get the other stools while the rest of the Gray Wolves stood there, making faces and laughing at us.

"We need to make nametags!" Orange Morning declared. She took a pile of yarn necklaces strung to construction paper cards off a hook and handed them around.

I stared at the orange construction paper, hanging from the red yarn; this was the moment of truth. Was I going to put "Noah" on the nametag, and have the Gray Wolves tease me? Or was I going to put "Bentley" on the nametag, and hope none of the Gray Wolves knew my real name? I waited to see what Chip would do. He wrote "CHIP" with a green crayon. Of course, he didn't write "Walter."

I wasn't sure how to spell "Bentley." I wrote, "BENTLY." Good enough. I put the yarn around my neck.

"Hey, I thought your name was Noah."

I looked up in horror. It was Justin. How did he know?

"Um . . ."

Crazy Alex laughed. He took an extra nametag off the table and drew a sloppy sailboat with some monkeys and giraffes on it. "Here you go. Fixed it." He slid it over to me as if I was going to put it on. "It's Noah's ark, get it?" Then he caught sight of Chip's nametag. "Chipmunk?" He and Justin thought that was hilarious. Chip just looked off into space, as if he didn't hear them.

"Chip-*munk!*" Crazy Alex repeated. "You know, the little squirrel?"

Chip continued to ignore him.

"A chipmunk isn't a squirrel," said Weatherman.

We all looked up, surprised that he would dare to say anything.

That's when Orange Morning came over to our table with some bark and wooly pieces of yarn. "Did I hear someone say they want to make a chipmunk? Hmm?"

Justin snickered and pointed to Chip. "He does!"

Chip shook his head but didn't say anything.

Orange Morning looked disappointed. "No? Well . . ." She put down her supplies in the center of the table. "I think this yarn would make really nice chip-munk fur if you want to give it a try." She clapped her hands together and spun around the room. "This is the time to experiment, as artists!"

After only a minute, Crazy Alex yelled that he was bored, and he and Justin walked out of the cabin.

"We have to do something," Chip whispered loudly.

"What? They just copied the map. And they have a cell phone. They could probably find the marsh-mallows on Google Earth," I said.

Mikey leaned in to hear us. "Hey, what are you guys talking about? I want to make a chipmunk."

"We're not making chipmunks," I said.

Harrison was back to reading his book

Weatherman leaned over the table. "Are you guys talking about the Navigation-off?"

"Yeah," I said.

"We have to win that," Weatherman said.

"Are you guys crazy?" Mikey said, loud enough for everyone in the room to look over at him.

"*Shhhhhh!*"

Orange Morning said something to Brian, who was busy on his cell phone, then he got up slowly and went outside to find Crazy Alex and Justin.

The other Gray Wolves were chucking the little pinecones at each other, and one of them was using a pair of open scissors to carve into their end of the table.

"FYI, the Gray Wolves took a picture of the map with their cell phone, so now they are for sure going to win," I whispered.

"That's not fair! What are we gonna do?" Mikey said, way too loudly.

"Mikey, stop shouting!" I shouted.

"But that's not fair!"

I leaned in. "No joke it's not fair, but—"

Crazy Alex and Justin shuffled back into the cabin, followed by their counselor Brian, playing an intense game on his cell phone. Crazy Alex looked at the fresh addition carved into the table and grabbed his stomach to let out a laugh. "Oh, this is classic! You gotta come see this!" he said, looking right at me.

I looked over my shoulder, wondering if he could be talking to somebody else.

Crazy Alex gestured with his index finger to come on over.

Chip got up, too, and we went over to have a look at what was so hilarious.

It was pretty hard to make out, but it looked like "LOSER OTTERS" had been carved into the arts and crafts table, forever.

"Oh, that's so funny," Chip said, rolling his eyes.

Mikey popped up from his chair. "I want to see something funny!"

Chip shook his head and tried to nudge Mikey back into his seat, but Mikey had to have a look.

"Looser Otters? I don't get it."

"It doesn't matter," Chip grumbled.

"Wow, learn to read," Crazy Alex said. "*Loser* Otters!" He grabbed the scissors and scratched another hilarious name into the table.

Justin put his face close to the table, squinting to make out the words. "I can't really see it."

"River Nerds! It says 'RIVER NERDS!' Ha, ha!"

"That's not as good as Loser Otters," said Justin.

Crazy Alex forced another laugh. "I think it's better!"

"What are we talking about over here, boys?" Orange Morning asked, smiling sweetly. "Are we brainstorming for project ideas? I think that's fantastic."

Chip sighed and sat back down. It was hopeless.

ॐ

Things were kind of quiet for the rest of the day. Even back in the cabin, nobody wanted to talk about what everyone was thinking. It started raining right after Dev had come in to announce, "Lights out!"

Harrison turned on his flashlight so he could continue reading.

Suddenly, from out of nowhere, Mikey asked, "Why'd you say that was 'so funny' if it wasn't funny?"

"I was being startastic," Chip said.

"What does that mean?" Mikey asked.

"It means . . . I meant the opposite of what I said."

"I think it's pronounced 'sarcastic,'" I said, and right away wished I hadn't.

"Whatever," Chip said. "Who cares."

"Why do we have to be losers and nerds?" Mikey asked. "Why can't we be cool winners?"

"I'm not a nerd or a loser," Chip said.

Plink. Plink. Plonk. Water was dripping on my head. I sat up. "You guys, I think the roof is leaking."

"That's what you get for taking the top bunk,"

Harrison said and went right back to his book.

I climbed down and tried to tug the whole bunk bed out of the way of the leak, but it wouldn't budge, especially with Harrison still on it. "Get up, Harrison. Somebody SOS Dev!"

Harrison reluctantly climbed out of his bed but continued reading with his flashlight.

"Gimme that!" Chip grabbed the flashlight away and started flashing it wildly out the window and into Dev's cabin window about thirty feet away.

Mikey and Weatherman got up to help push the bed, and we were starting to move it when Dev burst in, holding a bucket.

"The roof is leaking. On my head," I told him, as we shoved the bed into the middle of the room.

"Yeah," Dev nodded, "that happens." He put the bucket down to catch the drip. "What was going on with that flashlight? Were you guys trying to order pizza with Morse code?"

"It was SOS," Chip said.

Dev took the flashlight and demonstrated. "Three short, three long, three short."

"Whatever. You figured it out," said Chip.

"Yeah. I did. But I showed you how to do it so you could learn something." He handed the flashlight to Harrison, who jumped back into his bed to continue reading.

"I don't want to learn anything," Chip said.

"Me neither," said Mikey.

"Learning's for losers," I said.

Dev crossed his arms and looked around at all of us. "Well, at this camp, learning's for winners."

"I'd rather be cool," said Mikey.

"I knew this was summer school!" I said, crossing my arms back at Dev.

"It's not summer school," Dev said, "but if it was—"

"I knew it!" Chip shouted.

"Even if it was, which it isn't, how could anyone else be cooler than anyone else? Because you're all here. Right? You get me?"

Weatherman stopped mid-climb up to his bed. "I get it."

"I don't get it," said Mikey.

"I sort of get it," I said.

"Are you saying we're all in the dumb class, so none of us can be cool?" Chip asked.

"No, there's no such thing as a dumb class," Dev said, backing out of the room. "It doesn't matter about being cool anyway. I'm not cool. I don't care. Look, you guys should just try to win the Navigation-off. I think there's going to be a good prize—"

"Marshmallows! Hello!" Mikey yelled.

"Right, and I think the Navigation-off is considered a big deal. So, you'll really be, like, the top of the heap if you complete it."

"But, we can't," Mikey said.

Chip and I both shushed Mikey.

I shook my head at him.

Dev was almost out the door but stepped back in. "Why? What's going on?"

"Nothing," Chip and I said at the same time.

Dev shrugged. "Okay. Sounds like nothing. Whatever it is or it isn't, I know you guys can do it if you really try. Okay? 'night, you guys." He slipped out, closing the door as he went.

Chip glared at Mikey. "Why do you want to tell him?"

"Why not?" Mikey said. "It's not fair."

"But Mikey," I said, "if you tell on them for cheating, then they'll tell on us for cheating."

"But we didn't cheat," said Mikey. "Did we?" He wasn't so sure.

"No, but we won on accident," I said. "And they know that."

We all got back into our beds. I turned my pillow over so I could sleep on the dry side. The rain banged down harder on the roof, and it felt colder in the cabin.

"You guys," I said, "there has to be more than one map. Everybody can't have the same map."

"Yeah?" said Chip.

"So, what if they don't get that map?"

"Did you see the map?" asked Chip. "Would you know which one it was?"

"I don't know. I remember there was a big number four on it." I could hear the rain dripping into the bucket nearby.

"Okay, so, we can try to get that one," said Chip.

"Yeah," I said, but I didn't see how we'd have a choice.

CHAPTER 8
LOST IN THE MYSTERIOUS WOODS

"Wake up! Wake up! Rise and shine!" Dev shouted into our cabin. We heard the bugle a while ago, but it wasn't as loud as it had been before. It was easy to go back to sleep and ignore it.

"Today is tent-building day," he said.

"But today is Navigation-off," I said, rubbing my eyes.

"After tent-building," said Dev.

We didn't know what he was talking about until after breakfast, when Audrey and Steve announced that the three bunks that would be competing in today's "Tent-Building Challenge" were the River Otters, the Mallard Ducks, and, of course, the Gray Wolves.

"Every bunk has to do the Tent-Building Challenge," Audrey announced. She had on hiking boots and a huge backpack like she was about to go on a hike. Steve had on a big, floppy hat, and he also had a backpack, but it was little and had a long straw coming out of it that he was sipping on.

"What is that?" I asked Steve.

"Oh, this? This is my water bottle for hiking; only, it's not a bottle, it's a pouch. But I can carry a lot more water in it than in your average water bottle."

"Why do you need to carry so much water?"

"You should always carry lots of water when you go on a hike."

"Are you going on a hike?"

Steve looked around like he wasn't sure. "No . . . But I'm ready, just in case!"

Audrey swung open the door of a big old wooden shed she was standing in front of. "Okay, everybody, here's the rules. Each bunk has to pick one person to go into the shed and get the supplies you need to build a tent. You have exactly one minute to get everything you need. Then you have ten minutes to make a sturdy tent."

Mikey raised his hand.

"Yes, Mikey," Audrey said, pointing to him.

"What's the prize?"

Audrey smiled. "The prize is gaining the knowledge to survive in the wilderness."

"That's lame," Justin said loudly. The other Gray Wolves laughed.

"Why do we need to know how to survive in the wilderness?" Mikey asked. "Is that part of the Navigation-off?"

"No," said Audrey. "It's just good to have outdoor skills." She looked around at all our faces. Most of us weren't convinced. Except for the Mallard Ducks. Those guys started clapping and huddling up to make a plan like this was the greatest activity ever.

We huddled up.

"Does anyone know how to build a tent?" Chip asked.

We all looked at each other.

Mikey raised his hand. "I know how to make a fort out of blankets and couch pillows."

"Okay, so then, you get the stuff to build the tent."

Weatherman shook his head. "Shouldn't Noah do it? He figured out the scavenger hunt."

"So true," said Mikey. "Noah should do it."

"But—" Before I could get away, they pushed me right into the door of the shed.

Audrey was standing inside with a stopwatch. Crazy Alex from the Gray Wolves and a kid named Bradley from the Mallard Ducks were looking around the room at all the supplies.

"Three, two, one, GO!" Audrey said as she squeezed the stopwatch.

I didn't know what to do. Crazy Alex and Bradley were scrambling around the room, grabbing everything off the shelves and running toward the door.

"Where are you going, boys?" Audrey asked.

"To put this stuff outside," Bradley panted.

Audrey wagged her long index finger. "Once you leave the shed, you can't come back in."

Crazy Alex dumped all the supplies he'd collected onto the floor. "No way!"

I looked around and around, trying to figure out what in the world I could build a tent with. There were buoys attached to ropes, canoe paddles, life jackets, big baskets, shovels, boxes of garbage bags, boxes of popsicle sticks and construction paper, glue, magic markers, duct tape, candles, huge cans of tomatoes—there was so much stuff, but nothing that looked like a tent.

"You better start collecting supplies," Audrey told me.

"But I don't see anything to make a tent with."

Crazy Alex and Bradley were huffing and puffing and scrambling around, grabbing anything they could reach.

"Thirty seconds left!" Audrey announced.

Now I was starting to sweat. The rest of my bunk

was just outside the door, screaming, "Come on, Noah!"

Maybe I should get one of everything. I reached for a canoe paddle and a basket and put a bunch of small things in the basket.

"Fifteen seconds!" said Audrey.

My arms were hurting from trying to hold all the tent supplies. When I reached up to take a rolled-up net, that's when everything crashed to the floor.

The guys were screaming and waving their arms frantically.

I put everything I could fit into the basket and carried it outside.

"One second!"

Crazy Alex dove out of the shed and crashed onto the ground with his arms full of stuff. Bradley had so much stuff, half of it fell on the floor and didn't make it out of the shed.

"Time!" Audrey closed the shed door. "Wow, nice work, everyone. Now let's see what you can do."

I dropped all the stuff in a heap, and the guys gathered around.

Weatherman picked up the can of tomatoes. "What are we supposed to do with this?"

I shrugged. "I don't know. Maybe use it as a weight?"

"See!" Chip said, "I told you he knows what he's doing."

Audrey walked around the three groups. "Ten minutes!"

I rolled out the net. It was thick and heavy.

The Mallard Ducks had a box of trash bags they were rolling out. They also had duct tape. I wish I had grabbed the duct tape. You can make anything with that.

The Gray Wolves were sitting in a circle chucking their supplies at each other, and not building a tent.

"You guys, we need to put something over a tree branch," I said.

Mikey dug through the basket of stuff. "What do you mean?"

Chip was pretending he was in a canoe, paddling through the grass. "Like, build a fort?"

"Yeah," I said.

"There's a tree," said Weatherman, pointing to a maple tree with low branches.

I ran over to the tree and tried to throw the net over the lowest branch, but I just missed it. Chip ran over, and we tried throwing it together, but still couldn't reach. Finally, Weatherman walked over, balled up the net, and tossed it over the branch on his first try.

We stood around the net, dangling from the tree.

"Now what?" Weatherman asked.

Meanwhile, the Mallard Ducks were putting the

garbage bags they had taped together over a branch then holding down the sides with rocks.

The Gray Wolves were still throwing their supplies at each other.

"It's never going to work," Harrison declared as he came over and flopped down under the tree.

"If only they had couches and blankets, we could have done this no problem!" Mikey said, collapsing next to Harrison.

Chip pulled one side of the net out and put the canoe paddle on it to hold it down. I put the can of tomatoes and the basket with a box of popsicle sticks and a wrench on the other side.

"Okay, boys, time's up!" Audrey screeched.

First, she went to the Mallard Ducks. All the other campers gathered around.

"Well, this appears to be a tent," said Audrey. "Let's see what happens when you guys get in it."

The Mallard Ducks looked at each other, confused. Then, one by one, they got under their trash bag tent.

"That was a good idea finding rocks to hold down your tent. A tent is supposed to provide shelter. So, what happens when it rains?" Audrey picked up a watering can and sprinkled water on the tent.

The water rolled right off the garbage bags.

"Waterproof. Good job, boys!" Audrey said.

The Mallard Ducks crawled out from their tent, surprised that it had worked out so well.

Audrey carefully pulled the garbage bag tent off the branch, and then took the rope off the buoy. "You guys had a rope; that was one of the best things you could get," she said. She tied the rope around the trunk of the tree and held down the other end with the rocks. "There are so many ways to make a shelter."

Then Audrey walked over to our tent. "Okay, how about the River Otters?"

I looked at our volleyball net tent. Then I looked at Audrey's watering can.

"So, you need to get in there and see if it makes a good shelter," she said.

Chip shook his head. "No way, man."

Weatherman just stood there.

Harrison wasn't paying any attention.

Mikey crawled under the net. "Come on, Noah!" he said.

I looked over at the Gray Wolves, who had gathered around, waiting for the show to start. Justin and Crazy Alex were already laughing.

Audrey pointed her head in the direction of the tent. "Go on," she said.

I got down on the grass and crawled into the tent beside Mikey, who had a smile on his face like he didn't know what was about to happen.

"Let's see how this does," Audrey said. But then she tilted the watering can a little bit, so we only got splashed with a few drops of water.

The Gray Wolves booed and gave the thumbs down. They walked back to their heap of supplies and ignored the rest of Audrey's lesson.

"So we can see that this isn't waterproof material. What could we do if we were in the forest, and we had this net to make a tent? How could we make it a better shelter?" Audrey looked around. "Yes, Mikey?"

"Put trash bags on it?" he said.

"Okay. What if you didn't have trash bags? Maybe you could weave leaves and reeds into the netting? What about that?"

I shrugged.

Then Audrey walked over to the pile of supplies that was supposed to be the Gray Wolves' tent. "Where's your tent, guys?"

"It's right there," said Crazy Alex, pointing.

Audrey bent down to take a closer look at the messy pile of supplies. "I don't see it."

"Here."

"Where?"

"Right here!" Crazy Alex pointed to a can of beans on the ground.

Audrey got down on her knees and put on her reading glasses.

There, on top of the can, was a tiny tent made from a bent piece of metal.

"Oh, I see," she said. "Okay, get inside, and we'll test it out."

"That's not fair! You didn't say we had to make a tent we could all fit inside!" Crazy Alex said.

Audrey nodded. "Okay. How about just one of you?"

Crazy Alex picked up the mini tent and balanced it on top of his hair.

All the Gray Wolves laughed and clapped.

Audrey lifted her watering can to sprinkle Crazy Alex's head, but he jumped out of the way. "Hmmm. Looks like that doesn't do the job."

As soon as Audrey put the watering can down, Crazy Alex grabbed it and chased after the other Gray Wolves, trying to dump it on them.

Audrey didn't notice. "So, boys, if you were hiking deep into the wilderness, and you could only fit a few things in your backpack to pitch a tent, what would you absolutely need?"

I raised my hand. So did all the Mallard Ducks.

Audrey pointed to Bradley.

"Why couldn't you just buy a tent and bring it?" he asked.

Everybody started nodding and saying, "Yeah, that's what I was thinking."

"But what if you didn't have room in your backpack for a tent?"

I raised my hand again.

Right when Audrey pointed to me, the Gray Wolves charged up and dumped the watering can on my head. I screamed and ran away.

"What were you going to say, Noah?" Audrey called out.

The Gray Wolves laughed and high-fived each other.

I circled back and stood right next to Audrey so the Gray Wolves wouldn't dump water on me again. "Um, um, a rope?"

"Exactly! A rope and some kind of waterproof material, and you can make a tent anywhere!" Audrey exclaimed.

Weatherman raised his hand. "What if you're in the desert? And you can't find a tree?"

Everyone nodded again.

Audrey's mouth dropped open, but no answer came out. She looked at her watch. "You guys, we have to do the Navigation-off before lunch! We have to get going!"

All the bunks gathered outside Steve and Audrey's office for the big event of the day.

Justin from the Gray Wolves got a map and compass from Steve. He handed the map to Crazy Alex, who opened it up and started laughing. "Ha, ha!

Awesome!" He waved it around proudly and showed it to the rest of the Gray Wolves.

Chip and I looked at each other, thinking the same thing: the Gray Wolves just picked the map they took a picture of yesterday.

Then Steve handed me and Chip our map and compass. I didn't know what to do with either one. None of the River Otters did.

Crazy Alex came over and looked at our map. "Good luck, losers."

I folded the map up and put it under my shirt.

The rest of the Gray Wolves surrounded me.

"Don't get lost in the Mysterious Woods," Crazy Alex snickered.

Then Justin pointed his finger in my face. "And don't cheat!"

"Well," I stammered, "you shouldn't cheat either."

Audrey came over to us with her clipboard. "What's this about cheating?"

"Nothing," Chip said quickly.

"Okay, then," she said, looking suspiciously at the Gray Wolves. "Good luck, Otters!"

"Yeah, good luck!" Crazy Alex snapped. "And re-member . . . don't look up!"

The Gray Wolves laughed too hard like it was the funniest thing they'd ever heard in their lives.

All the different bunks ran in every direction as

if the Navigation-off was a race or something. We started running, too, only, we didn't know where we were going.

The next thing we knew we were standing by the shores of Mudd Lake. Dev was following way behind us because we weren't supposed to ask for help. But we needed help, like crazy.

Off in the distance, the Gray Wolves were strolling along, drinking juice boxes and pulling leaves off the trees. They saw us and stopped in their tracks so they could all point and laugh.

"Why are they laughing at us?" Mikey whispered.

"I don't know," I said. I held up the map, pretending I knew what we were doing.

Chip took the map out of my hands and gave me the compass. "Let me see."

Mikey took the compass out of my hand and shook it. "How do we know the battery's not dead?"

"I don't think there's a battery," said Weatherman.

"Then it's for sure not working," said Mikey.

I was turning around in circles, holding the map, trying to figure out which direction we had to go. Chip turned in the opposite direction, watching the arrow rotate.

"This is stupid," Harrison grumbled. "All this work for a bag of marshmallows?"

There was a big letter "N" at the top of the map,

and there was an "N" on the compass.

I took the compass back from Chip. Then I turned around and faced Mudd Lake. We were only a few steps from the water. "It says to go this way." I pointed to the lake. "Fifty feet." I started to pace off, "One, two, three . . ."

Mikey followed me.

"If we go fifty feet that way, we'll be under the water!" Chip screamed. He went after me and grabbed the compass. He held it steady. "Look, the arrow's pointing to the N. That means that's north."

"I know," I said, standing in the water.

"So make the N on the map go the same way."

I held the map next to the compass, so both had N at the top. "We were totally going the wrong way!"

"No wonder the Gray Wolves were laughing at us," said Chip.

"No wonder the lake was in the way," said Weatherman.

"No wonder the map was all wrong," said Mikey.

We started to walk into the Mysterious Woods. We were getting farther and farther away from camp and deeper and deeper into the woods. We could still see Dev trailing behind us. He said he was there just in case we got lost.

"Do you guys know where we are?" Weatherman asked.

"We're in the woods, duh," said Harrison, who was trying to read a book while following us.

"We're in the Mysterious Woods," said Chip.

We all stopped walking at the same time and looked up.

"We're not supposed to look up!" Mikey screamed.

We all looked down.

"At least one person should look up at all times to make sure the Zombie Crow isn't watching us," Chip said. "I think it should be Harrison because he's not helping anyway."

Harrison went back to reading his book. "No, I'm busy."

We kept walking.

I looked from the map to a huge, square boulder up ahead. "You guys, look! That looks like this!" I pointed to the map.

"Glacial boulder," Chip read.

"What's a glacier boulder?" asked Mikey.

Chip and I both pointed to the giant rock.

The map showed a tree thirty feet to the west of the "glacial boulder." We got to the boulder and then turned and started walking.

"How do we know when it's thirty feet?" Mikey asked.

There were trees all around us. From the map, it looked like there would be just one big tree. "How do we know which tree it is?"

"How indeed," said a voice.

We looked back. There was an old man leaning against the boulder, holding a wooden walking stick.

I let out a scream. "The Zombie Crow!"

The old man looked around. "What? No. I'm Steve's uncle, Alden." He waved to Dev, who was off in the distance.

"Steve, the guy who runs our camp?" I asked.

"Hey, Uncle Alden," Dev said, waving back.

"Are you looking for the marshmallows, too?" Mikey asked.

The old man stood straight. "Huh? Marshmallows? I'm looking for pirate treasure. Thought that's what you were doing with that map."

"Pirate treasure?"

"Woah!"

Everyone gathered around the old man.

"Why would pirates bury treasure way out here?" I asked.

"Yeah, don't they live on ships? In the ocean?"

"That's true, but there were some clever pirates who wanted to hide their treasure where no one would think to look for it," said the old man. "Trouble is, one day, they came back to dig it up, and couldn't find it."

Mikey crossed his arms. "How do you know? Are you a pirate?"

"No, but I used to run this camp with Steve's father, my brother Walt."

"Does Steve know about the pirate treasure?"

"Of course."

"Why didn't he tell us about it?"

"I don't know," said Uncle Alden. "Maybe he gave up on it."

"Really?"

"Sure. But I won't stop searching until I find it," he declared. He looked over my shoulder at the map. "So, what are you boys looking for?"

"We need to find this tree," I said.

"That's where the marshmallows are," said Mikey.

Great-Uncle Alden looked at the tree on the map. "Well, I'd say you went in exactly the wrong direction."

"But it says thirty feet from the 'glacier deposit,'" I said.

"This glacial deposit right here?"

"Yeah."

"It says to go west. You went east."

Chip held the compass up next to the map, making sure north was going in the same direction on both. "Oh, yeah. Okay, let's go." Chip started walking.

"No way, we need to find the pirate treasure first!" Mikey said.

Uncle Alden laughed. "I've been looking for fifty years."

"First the marshmallows, then the pirate treasure," I said.

Uncle Alden nodded. "Good luck, boys. Hope it doesn't take you fifty years to find the marshmallows."

We counted off thirty steps from the boulders, this time heading west. Right in front of us was a big tree.

I saw a piece of paper attached to the front of the tree. "Look, a note!"

Mikey was walking around the tree in search of the marshmallows.

I took the note off the tree and opened it up. It was another map! "Oh, no!"

"Where are the marshmallows?!" Mikey cried.

Everyone gathered around to look at the new map. Just then, big drops of rain started plopping onto the map. The ink started to run. I folded it back up and stuffed it in my pocket.

We were deep in the woods, far from our cabin, and the rain was falling harder and harder.

"What do we do now?" I said.

Then I watched as Weatherman pulled his folded-up rain poncho out of his backpack and put it on.

"Hey, why didn't you tell us it was going to rain?" asked Chip.

Weatherman pulled up his hood. "I forgot."

I saw Dev waving for us to follow him. "It's always raining here," I grumbled.

When we caught up to Dev, he gave Weatherman the thumbs up for having a rain poncho. "Looks like part two of the Navigation-off will have to wait until tomorrow."

"What about the marshmallows?" Mikey cried.

Harrison was still reading his book, even though the pages were getting soaked by the rain. "Yeah, that's not fair."

"Don't you guys want to get inside and dry off?" Dev asked.

"I want to find the pirate treasure," I said.

BOOOOOOMMM!

CHAPTER 9
FINDING A MAP

Not anymore, I didn't. That was thunder.

We started running. We didn't need the map to find our way back. It turns out that Dev knew where we were going all along. Dev knows his way all around the camp.

We ran to the dining hall, getting totally soaked in the downpour (except Weatherman, of course). Dev said there would probably be hot cocoa (without marshmallows) when we got there. We ran so fast, we thought for sure we'd be the first ones there. But that was the weird thing. The Gray Wolves happened to be there already, sitting around their table, drinking hot cocoa . . . and they were completely dry!

They looked up at us when we burst through the door.

"Did you guys fall in the lake?" Crazy Alex asked.

The other Gray Wolves laughed so hard, some of them sprayed hot cocoa on each other.

"It's raining," Weatherman said, taking off his poncho.

"Duh," said Chip.

Justin stood up and stalked toward Chip. "We know it's raining," he hissed.

Chip backed up nervously, stepping on my foot.

"Well, that's how we got wet," I stammered, hopping back before my other foot got stepped on.

"No duh," said Justin, turning his glare on me.

Dev had gone into the kitchen to get our cocoa. Why was he never around when the Gray Wolves were bothering us?

"Where are your marshmallows?" Crazy Alex asked.

"Um, we didn't find them yet," I said.

The Gray Wolves were circling around us now like we were their prey.

"You're never gonna find them," Crazy Alex cackled. "They don't want you guys to have marshmallows, so they make it impossible to find them."

Mikey let out a gasp. "Really?!"

Just then Dev came out of the kitchen with a tray of hot cocoa for us. The Gray Wolves' counselor was with him.

Crazy Alex looked at the counselors and then to

us and just shrugged like he couldn't say anymore.

We sat down at our table to get away from the Gray Wolves.

"If it stops raining after lunch, we can go back out and do the rest of the Navigation-off," said Dev.

"But," Mikey said, glancing back at the Gray Wolves, "nobody can find the marshmallows."

Dev passed out the cocoa. "What?"

"It's impossible," Harrison said.

"It's not impossible," said Dev. "Steve and Audrey wouldn't do that. They want you to find it."

"They do?"

"Of course, they do."

I looked back at Crazy Alex, who was laughing and pointing at us.

After lunch, the sun was back out, so we headed for the tree where we found the second map. It was a lot easier getting there this time since we'd already figured it out. The first thing we did was line up the map with NORTH on the compass.

"You guys, we just gotta find those marshmallows," Mikey said.

"We will," said Chip.

"We probably won't," said Harrison. He didn't look up from his book.

"We found the second map, didn't we?" said Chip.

"Yeah, but where are all the other teams?"

"How would you even know where the other teams are, Harrison? You can't see them because you're always looking at your book!"

Chip had a point there.

"I don't get what happened," I said. "If the Gray Wolves got the map they took a picture of, why didn't they find their marshmallows?"

"Maybe it's true, maybe it's impossible," said Chip.

I was holding the map. "It says to go twenty yards southwest until you reach a big X."

"X marks the spot!" Mikey screamed.

"How are we supposed to know what a 'yard' is?" I asked.

"Football," said Weatherman.

Chip nodded. "Yeah, they have yards in football."

"Okay, so how far is it?" I asked.

We all looked at Weatherman.

He shrugged. "I don't know."

We looked at Dev, who was leaning against a tree, somewhere nearby.

"Is there an asterisk?" asked Dev.

Chip pointed to the little star thing next to the word "yards."

"Yeah?"

"So look for the asterisk at the bottom of the page," said Dev.

In tiny print at the bottom of the map was another

asterisk. "It says, 'A yard is three feet.'"

"Three times twenty is sixty," said Weatherman.

We counted out sixty steps, trying to go south-west according to the compass.

When we got to sixty, there wasn't a big "X."

"Ow!"

We looked to our left. Harrison had drifted off course from us because he was reading his book and ended up walking into two trees that crossed each other.

"You guys, look!" Chip shouted, running over to Harrison. "X!"

We gathered around the trees.

"Wow, how'd they do that?" Mikey asked. He put one hand on each tree that made the big X.

Harrison was still rubbing his head after banging into the X. "I don't see any marshmallows," he said.

"Oh, no!" I said, pulling a piece of folded paper off the center of the X. "I hope it's not another map."

I opened the paper. On it was a picture of a bag of marshmallows, and the words: "Congratulations! This voucher is good for a marshmallow campfire."

"What's a voucher? Where are the marshmal-lows?" Mikey asked.

Suddenly, Dev appeared out of nowhere. "They can't put the marshmallows in the woods or the ani-mals will get them. So they put a voucher. You bring the voucher back to camp, and they'll give you a bag of marshmallows."

Mikey flopped down on the ground. "But I'm hungry."

Dev pulled a granola bar out of his pocket. "You can have this."

Mikey waved it off. "Gross."

"Okay . . ."

"Wait—" Mikey took it and stuffed it into his mouth.

CHAPTER 10
FACE-OFF

We were all starving by the time we got back to camp. Audrey said we couldn't have our marshmallows until after supper, and then we could toast them with the other winners. I guess Audrey decided that having marshmallows was too much good food for one day, so they served us fish for supper. *Fish*. Not even fish sticks, but actual chunks of plain, white fish. It looked so bad Mikey accidentally ate a piece of broccoli.

ॐ

There were two campfires outside, for the bunks that had found their marshmallow vouchers. We all got sticks and marshmallows and were about to put them in the fire when Audrey and Steve came over.

"How's it going, guys?" Steve asked.

"Good."

"Do you guys know how to toast marshmallows?"

We all looked at each other. Who doesn't know how to toast a marshmallow?

"Yeah . . ."

"Good. Nice work today. I think you had one of the more challenging maps."

"Your uncle helped us," I said quickly.

Weatherman looked from me to Steve. "That's okay, right?"

"Sure, it is. That's called being resourceful. When you're navigating in the woods, you may come across other hikers, and they can help you."

Then I remembered what else Uncle Alden told us. "He said he was looking for pirate treasure. Can we go look for it, too?"

Steve winked at Audrey. "Maybe as a special prize for your bunk, if you win the Quiz Bowl."

"What's the Quiz Bowl?" I asked.

"I guess you'll have to stick around to find out," said Steve.

The way he said that sounded like he knew I wasn't sure I wanted to stay at camp.

Meanwhile, Mikey was toasting his marshmallow, and it wasn't just toasted—it was on fire. He waved the stick in the air, and the marshmallow stopped burning. But it was totally black. He held it up proudly. "Awesome!"

Harrison's marshmallow was still white when it fell into the fire. "That's not fair. This stick isn't good."

"Haven't you guys ever toasted marshmallows?" I asked. Sure, I'd never been to camp before, but if there's one thing I know, it's how to toast a marshmallow. "Look." I held up my marshmallow. "You put it almost all the way through," I stuffed it onto the stick, "and then you hold it like this." I put the marshmallow in the top part of the flames. "So you don't get ash on it or burn it." I turned it slowly, so it got brown all around and then held it up for everyone to see. "Now it's all crispy on the outside and squishy on the inside."

Everyone watched me bite my marshmallow.

Weatherman held his marshmallow out. "Can you make mine?"

"Yeah, can you toast mine?" All the other guys asked.

That's when the Gray Wolves came by with empty marshmallow sticks in their hands.

"Give us some of your marshmallows," Justin ordered.

They looked so much bigger than us, standing over us, the glow of the fire on their faces. Harrison started to hand the whole bag to them.

"No, don't give it to them!" Chip said.

But it was too late; Crazy Alex grabbed the bag out of Harrison's hand, and all the Gray Wolves started taking marshmallows.

"That's not fair. Eat your own marshmallows!" Chip shouted.

Crazy Alex shrugged. "We don't have any. But that's not our fault. That Navigation-off was the worst thing *ever*."

All of the Gray Wolves took a marshmallow, and Justin took two. "We don't need to find it," he said. "We can just take yours."

Crazy Alex saw Dev coming, so he dropped the bag of marshmallows on the ground, and all the Gray Wolves ran away.

There were still enough marshmallows for us each to have one more. Everyone watched me demonstrate how to toast a marshmallow to crispy brown perfection.

"You guys," I said, "if they never found their voucher, then it's still out there."

"Do you think if we found it, we could have their bag of marshmallows?" asked Weatherman.

"But how would we get their map?" Chip asked.

Mikey's marshmallow had caught on fire again, and he was waving it around wildly. "They probably won't give it to us."

"We should check the trash," I said. "They probably threw it away."

"Gross, I'm not looking in the trash," said Harrison.

"Wait," said Weatherman, "didn't we have to give the maps back?"

We asked Dev if he could get the map from Audrey and Steve. He shrugged his shoulders and went off to ask them, and then came back with the map in his hands.

"Nobody ever thought of doing that before," he said proudly.

Crazy Alex and Justin, followed by the rest of the Gray Wolves, came charging back when they saw that we had their map.

"That's not fair!" Crazy Alex screamed.

"Yeah!" said Justin.

Steve and Audrey came over.

"What's going on, boys?" Audrey asked.

"It's not fair that they get our marshmallows," said Crazy Alex.

"Nobody has the marshmallows yet," said Audrey.

"Would you still like to find the marshmallows?" asked Steve.

All the Gray Wolves nodded.

"Okay," said Steve. "I have another map, a different map that goes to the same destination point. The River Otters can have a map, and the Gray Wolves can have a map. Whichever team gets to the destination point first wins the marshmallows. Okay?"

"Still not fair," said Crazy Alex, folding his arms.

"Do you want the old map or the new map?" Steve asked the Gray Wolves.

"The new map," said Justin.

"But it could be harder," said Crazy Alex.

"But the old map's impossible," said Justin. The other Gray Wolves agreed.

Crazy Alex looked up at Steve. "We'll take the new map."

"Okay, come with me," said Steve.

As the Gray Wolves were walking away, Crazy Alex turned back and said, "Good luck, losers!"

That night, I wrote another letter to my parents.

> Dear Mom and Dad:
> Today we had to find marshmallows. We had a map and a compass. It was hard. We kept going in the wrong direction. Steve's uncle told us there is pirate treasure in the

woods. That makes me want to stay in camp to find the treasure. We found the marshmallows. It wasn't marshmallows, but a piece of paper that says we can have marshmallows. We toasted marshmallows at the campfire. I am the best at toasting marshmallows. But then the Gray Wolves took our marshmallows away because they didn't find theirs. That's not fair. All the guys were mad. The Gray Wolves are mean and are ruining camp. Then we got their navigation map. We can find their marshmallows and have more marshmallows now. They also got a map, so we have to find the marshmallows first.

It is really dark at night. I am kind of scared because they said there was a Zombie Crow that attacks people. I am not sure I want to stay at camp because of this. I will let you know. If we can find the marshmallows and the pirate treasure tomorrow, then maybe I can come home, and I won't need to stay at camp.

Love,
Noah

CHAPTER 11
RIVER OTTERS VS. GRAY WOLVES

This was it—the big day. We were going head to head against the Gray Wolves to find their marshmallows. I was actually kind of nervous.

"What if the map is impossible?" asked Harrison.

"What if the Zombie Crow is guarding the marshmallows?" asked Mikey.

"What if we are losers?" asked Weatherman.

These were all good questions.

"How can we be losers if we found the marshmallows yesterday, and they didn't?" asked Chip.

That was a good question, too.

"But what if their map *is* impossible?" asked Harrison.

"What if the Zombie Crow—"

"Stop it!" Chip yelled.

&

When we got to the dining hall for breakfast, the Gray Wolves were nowhere in sight.

"See, you guys, the Gray Wolves aren't even awake yet!" said Chip.

A Mallard Duck (not a real duck; one of the guys in the Mallard Duck cabin) who was at our table said, "They were here before. They left already."

We looked at each other in a panic.

"Are you serious?" Chip yelled. "For real?"

"They're already looking for the marshmallows!" I screamed. They were going to beat us! I jumped up from the table. "We have to go!"

Mikey was calmly pouring his second bowl of cereal. "I'm not going anywhere."

"No, come on!" I said.

"You should eat your breakfast first," said Dev.

"Exactly," said Mikey. "Breakfast is the second most important meal of the day. After lunch and supper."

I wasn't hungry. I wanted to get out there and find those marshmallows before the Gray Wolves.

Dev spread jelly on a piece of toast and looked around at all of us. "You know the story about the race between the tortoise and the hare?"

Mikey stopped chewing. "Hair?"

"A rabbit," said Dev.

"What?"

"A hare is another word for rabbit."

"Oh," said Mikey. Then he stopped chewing again. "A rabbit and a tortoise in a race? The rabbit's gonna win."

"In this story, the tortoise wins," said Dev, "because slow and steady wins the race."

Mikey shook his head. "I don't think so."

"It's not a true story," said Dev. "It's a life lesson."

"A lesson on how to lose," said Mikey.

"Mikey's right!" I yelled. "Slow is for losers!" I was going crazy just sitting there, while the Wolves were probably seconds from finding the marshmallow voucher.

"What about, 'The early bird catches the worm'?" said Weatherman.

"Yeah!" That was a good one. I wish I'd thought of that.

"Worms are gross," said Harrison from behind his book.

"I'm not leaving until I've had breakfast," said Dev.

I sat back down. "I really think we should get going," I pleaded.

Chip chugged down a glass of orange juice. "They had the whole day to find it yesterday, and they didn't. Right?"

"But they have a different map today," I said. "And it's probably a lot easier."

It seemed like *forever* before we finally got outside and opened up the map, which had mud stains and dead bugs on it.

The first thing we did was figure out which direction we needed to go.

I pointed in the direction of the woods on the other side of the field.

"That can't be right," said Chip. "We saw the Gray Wolves in the woods yesterday, and that was in the opposite direction."

"Maybe they messed up so bad they went the wrong way when they started," I said.

"The total wrong way?" asked Chip.

The rest of the team looked at the map and the compass.

"It says, 'Two hundred paces due south of the dining hall door,'" I read.

We faced south and started to pace off two hundred steps.

We ended up just inside the woods, on the other side of the field.

"This is where we had the scavenger hunt," said

Mikey. He was right.

Harrison was still pacing since he was in the middle of a book.

"Harrison, stop!" we all screamed, just before he walked into another tree.

He looked up, surprised to see a huge tree in front of him. When he turned around, he started pointing at someone across the field. "Look! You guys!"

We could see Justin from the Gray Wolves running in the opposite direction. It looked like he was going toward the Mysterious Woods.

I shook my head in frustration. "He was spying on us!"

"He's probably going to tell the Gray Wolves where we are!" said Chip.

"I bet they went the wrong way again," I said.

"Hurry! We have to find the marshmallows!" Mikey screamed, flapping his arms around.

Chip and I looked at the map.

"Our first landmark is a hollowed-out tree trunk," I said.

Weatherman stood in one place and slowly turned in a circle. "There," he said, pointing to a big hollow log not far from us.

We ran over to it.

"Okay, okay, now what?" Mikey yelled.

"Twenty paces south," I read.

Chip and I were practically experts at using the compass by now.

Everyone took twenty big steps.

"Now what?" asked Weatherman.

Harrison had decided to sit down on the hollow log and get back to reading his book.

"Come on, Harrison!" Mikey called.

But Harrison didn't budge.

"If you're going to just sit there, why don't you be on the lookout for the Gray Wolves?" said Chip.

"Hey, that's a good idea," I said. "You be the lookout!"

Harrison nodded, but he didn't look like he was listening.

We kept going deeper and deeper into the woods, following the directions on the map. Dev was somewhere nearby, and we could still see Harrison because he was wearing a red shirt, but we were getting farther and farther away from him.

The next part of the navigation instructions was really weird.

"It says, 'Find the Old Man's Beard.'"

The other guys gathered around to see the instructions for themselves.

"The Old Man's Beard?" Weatherman asked.

"Okay, I'm very serious, you guys," Mikey said, looking around, a little panicky. "Is there an old man out here? With a beard?"

That's when we heard shouts of: "There they are!" and "I see them!" coming from somewhere in the woods.

CHAPTER 12
THE HIDDEN CABIN

"They're coming!" I screamed. "We have to find the Old Man's Beard!"

"I don't even get what the Old Man's Beard is!" Chip screamed.

We could see the Gray Wolves winding through the trees, getting closer and closer.

"Oh, no! Do something!" yelled Mikey.

I looked at the map again. "It says, 'Old Man's Beard is a kind of leechen...'"

Weatherman looked over my shoulder. "It says it's pronounced 'liken.'"

"'And it usually grows on the north side of trees around here.'" I looked at Chip. "So we have to find it on the north side of a tree."

"But which tree?" Mikey asked.

The Gray Wolves were charging toward us, pointing and waving their map. Now we couldn't do anything until they got away from us, because otherwise, they'd just follow us.

The six of them practically crashed into us, panting and sweating from all the running they had just done.

"Did—you—find—the—marshmallows—yet?" Crazy Alex asked, doubled over and out of breath.

"No," I said, trying not to sound nervous.

"Good, because you're not going to," said Justin, laughing.

All the Gray Wolves stopped panting so they could laugh really hard like they'd just heard the funniest thing in the world.

"It must be nearby," said Crazy Alex. "All we have to do now is look for a bag of marshmallows."

"It's not—" Mikey started to explain (about the voucher being in place of the bag of marshmallows), but Chip gave him a little kick. "Ow!"

"It's not what?" asked Crazy Alex.

Chip and I looked at each other in a panic. "Uh, it's not around here," said Chip. "We already looked."

Crazy Alex tipped his head like he didn't believe what we were saying. "Then why are you guys here if it's not around here?"

"Yeah," said Justin.

"We have to follow the map," I said.

Crazy Alex squinted his eyes, then turned away and looked at his map along with some of the other Gray Wolves. He was holding the compass, and it looked like he had figured out how to use it.

Meanwhile, we huddled up by a tree to get away from them, but Justin was still standing over us as if he had decided to join our group.

"How are we going to find it now with them here?" Chip whispered loudly.

I looked back at the Gray Wolves, who had started walking away, with Crazy Alex leading them. "They're going. I guess they figured it out."

Justin hurried after them.

That's when Harrison came running through the woods, waving his arms wildly. "You guys! The Gray Wolves know where you are!"

"Yeah, they found us," said Chip.

I was desperately looking around again for the tree with Old Man's Beard growing on it.

"Hey, how did you find us so easily?" Chip asked Harrison.

"I could see you."

Weatherman was helping me look for the beard. "Which way is north?" he asked.

Chip had the compass. He pointed north.

Weatherman waved us over to a tree he'd found.

"How do you know that's a lichen?" Mikey asked.

It looked like a bunch of greenish beard hairs hanging from the side of the tree.

"Gross!" Harrison yelled when he saw it.

"I think that's it," I whispered, peeking around the tree to see if the Wolves were within earshot. "It looks like a beard, doesn't it?"

"Yeah!" Mikey said, high fiving everybody.

Chip looked behind us. "*Shhh.* You don't want them to hear."

We could see them, off in the distance, pacing down a hill to the east.

Our next step was to find an old cabin exactly northeast of the Old Man's Beard.

"A whole cabin? How hard could that be to find?" asked Chip.

"This is it, you guys," I said. "This is the last place we have to go."

"When you say, 'cabin,' do you mean a real cabin or a cabin made out of lichen?" Mikey asked.

"That's a good question," said Chip.

I looked at him like he was nuts. "Is it?"

Mikey was standing there, with his hands on his hips. "Well? What's the answer?"

"It's a real cabin!" I shouted.

"*Shhh*! We have to hurry!" Chip scolded.

I focused on the map. Harrison didn't go back to reading his book. Chip held the compass steady, so we would know exactly which way was northeast. Weatherman scanned the woods for signs of the Gray Wolves.

"Maybe we should scrunch down," said Harrison.

"What do you mean?" I asked.

"Yeah," said Chip. "Harrison could see us when he was far away. If we get down . . ." Chip scrunched down low, "maybe they won't see us."

We all scrunched down, like we were hiding behind a desk, and started creeping, northeast, little by little, like turtles, between the trees. It was slow going and hard to do. The weird thing was, all I could see ahead of us were more trees. We kept going.

"What if we're going in the wrong direction?" I asked.

"Northeast from the Old Man's Beard," said Chip.

"Yeah, and where are the Gray Wolves?" asked Mikey. "Maybe they already found it."

Dev was way behind us, looking at his cellphone.

"I wish Dev could help us," said Harrison.

"Let's go fifty more paces, and if we don't see anything, we go back to the Old Man's Beard," I said.

So we went, forty-eight, forty-nine, fifty. We stopped, and I got behind a tree so I could stand up tall and look far ahead of us. There was no cabin in sight. Mikey decided to stand up, too.

"Nothing!" Mikey declared, scanning the whole area.

"Mikey, get down!" Chip whispered.

SUMMER CAMP ACADEMY

"That wasn't really fifty paces," I said, "because our steps aren't as big because we're scrunched down." I was about to say we should go a little farther when Mikey screamed.

"Oh, no! The Gray Wolves!" (How many times had I heard that today?)

Everyone popped up now to have a look at the Gray Wolves coming from the south. They stopped at a group of big stumps before continuing directly toward us.

"Keep looking!" Chip hollered.

We paced a few steps forward. I looked and looked, but didn't see a cabin. We must have navigated so badly that we weren't anywhere near the cabin! How messed up could we be not to see a whole cabin standing in the middle of the woods. I mean, how hard could it be to find a WHOLE CABIN?

Then I saw it.

"Look!" I said, pointing at a heap of brown, rotten wood in a square shape right near us. It was a tiny old cabin that had fallen down on the ground.

"*Shhh!*" said Chip.

But it was too late. The Gray Wolves saw me pointing and started running toward us.

We ran to the cabin and looked all around. All we could see were old, moss-covered pieces of wood.

"Maybe there's another cabin!" Mikey screamed.

The Gray Wolves had almost reached us.

We searched around the entire cabin for any sign of the voucher.

I felt like my heart was in my throat. I could hardly breathe. The Gray Wolves were about to show up and ruin everything. They were about to win the marshmallows, and laugh and point at us and tell us we were losers. I don't know why it bothered me so much, but it did. It really, really did.

Then I saw it: an old wooden box that said "mail" sitting in a pile of dead leaves next to the cabin. I let out a gasp. And picked it up.

"But that could be somebody's mailbox," said Mikey. "You can't open that."

"I don't think anybody lives here," said Chip.

I couldn't speak. I started to open the old mailbox when BAM! The Gray Wolves ran right into us. Then Justin knocked the mailbox out of my hands!

The mailbox fell open, and there, tucked inside, was a little piece of folded white paper.

Justin picked up the mailbox and angrily dumped the folded paper onto the ground. "Where are the marshmallows?" he yelled.

I quickly picked up the piece of paper and unfolded it.

"It's the voucher!" Mikey said, jumping up and down.

"What's a voucher?" asked Justin.

Crazy Alex came up and grabbed the voucher out of my hands. He read, "Congratulations! This voucher is good for a marshmallow campfire."

"Told you it was the voucher!" Mikey said, continuing to jump around.

"I don't get it," said Crazy Alex. He started looking around the cabin pile for the marshmallows.

"Give us back the voucher. We found it first," said Chip.

"Yeah, that's not fair," said Harrison.

I started to feel so mad. I couldn't believe it. We found the voucher, for real, and the Gray Wolves just took it away from us. I looked around for Dev. He was leaning against a tree, watching the whole thing.

All the Gray Wolves were lifting up pieces of wood and looking under them for the marshmallows. None of them understood what the voucher was.

So maybe there was still a chance we could get the voucher back, but how?

CHAPTER 13
LOST AND FOUND

I waved the other River Otters over for a huddle. None of the guys wanted to walk away from the cabin, but I kept waving until they all did.

"This better be good," said Chip.

"What difference does it make? They already have the voucher," Harrison whined.

"We're going to get the voucher back," I said. "I have a plan."

"It's too late," said Weatherman, looking back at the Gray Wolves.

"We have to try," I said.

"Yeah!" Mikey cheered quietly.

❧

When we broke up from the huddle, the guys spread out around the cabin. They each stood next to a Gray Wolf and pretended to be searching for the marshmallows alongside them.

Justin shoved Chip. "I'm looking here, cheater!"

I stood next to Crazy Alex and pretended to be looking under a big plank of wood. "I think I see the marshmallows!" I said.

Crazy Alex pushed me aside and grabbed the plank to lift it up. The voucher fell out of his hand.

I picked it up and started running. "I got it!" I yelled.

All the River Otters ran after me.

When the Gray Wolves figured out what happened, they ran after us.

We ran as fast as we could through the woods, and we weren't even sure we were going in the right direction. We ran and ran. Mikey was way behind. "You guys, wait up!" he shouted.

Then, as I was running so fast the trees were a blur, I saw something red on the ground. I stopped so suddenly, Weatherman slammed into me. It was my yo-yo! The one I lost the first day of camp!

"My yo-yo!" I grabbed it, but the string was caught on a big root poking out of the ground. The

Gray Wolves were catching up. I yanked on the yo-yo string, and, as I did, a long root rose up from the ground. I tugged and pulled; the root must have been about ten feet long! Then, one by one, the Gray Wolves tripped on the root. We got away!

"They're coming! Run!" Chip screamed.

We ran and ran, and we almost got to the steps of the main office when Crazy Alex tackled me, and the next thing I knew, we were all in a big heap on the grass with the Gray Wolves pig-piled on top of us.

"*Owww!*" I yelled from under everyone.

"Who has the voucher?" Chip asked from somewhere in the pile.

We scrambled around, trying to find the voucher. Everything was on the ground now—the maps, the compasses, hats, someone's sneaker . . .

Chip and I saw the voucher and crawled over to it. There was a torn piece of map on top of it. We looked at each other with the same idea.

Chip jumped to his feet and screamed, "I found it!" and started running for the office door. All the Gray Wolves grabbed him.

That's when I made my move, sprinting past the Gray Wolves and bursting into the office.

Steve and Audrey were at their desks.

I slapped the paper down. "We—found—the—voucher," I said, out of breath.

Mikey came in huffing and puffing and collapsed onto the floor.

Audrey popped up. "Are you okay, Mikey?"

"Too—much—running," he said, staring up at the ceiling.

"How about a glass of water?" said Audrey.

"Need—marshmallows—now," said Mikey.

The rest of the River Otters and the Gray Wolves came into the office. Chip gave me a high-five.

"Congratulations, River Otters!" Steve said. "Looks like it was a close contest!" He pulled a bag of marshmallows out of the desk drawer.

Crazy Alex opened his mouth to protest.

"Did you want to say something, Alex?" asked Steve.

"Grrrrr," he said, glaring at me.

"'Grrrrr' isn't very sportsman-like," said Audrey.

"Shake hands, boys," said Steve. "I'm sure everyone did their best."

Some of the Gray Wolves shook hands with us, but Crazy Alex put his hand out for me to shake and then took it away before I could. "Next time, cheaters," he whispered.

We ran out of the office with the winning bag of marshmallows and saw Dev and the Gray Wolves' counselor, Brian, walking across the field toward the office.

"Dev, we won!" Chip screamed.

"I know. I saw," he said.

&

After that, we finally got to go in the water! And there wasn't a cloud in the sky. Dev told us we had to stay in the shallow section until we passed the swimming test to go in the deeper water. This was bad because the shallow water was muddy and filled with bark and pine cones. I saw some of the guys from the older bunks who had been in camp last year, jumping off the raft in the "Advanced Swimmers" section.

"Mud Lake," Chip said, splashing muddy water in my face.

I splashed him back. "That's why it's called Mudd Lake."

Harrison sat down in the mud, staring out at the guys on the raft. "It's not fair. How come they get to be in the fun water?"

"Just pass the swim test, and you can be out there, too," Dev said. He was standing on the shore, rubbing sunscreen on his face.

Mikey showed up with an orange lifejacket on and splashed down in the mud. "I know how to swim."

"When can we take the test?" I asked.

Dev checked the clipboard he was always carrying around. "Not until Monday."

"Whaaat?" Chip and I said at the same time.

Weatherman found an innertube and was floating around, smiling. "It doesn't matter how deep the water is if you can float," he said.

That's when we all pounced on him, and the innertube sunk right down to the squishy bottom.

∞

Dear Mom and Dad:

Tomorrow I get to call you and tell you if I want to stay at camp or I want you to pick me up. I'm still thinking. Here's what happened today: I found my yo-yo! We did another Navigation-off. We found the voucher for the marshmallows before the Gray Wolves did. We had the best s'mores ever. We let the Gray Wolves have some marshmallows because they never found them. Maybe they will stop being mean.

We got to go swimming. Yay! They won't let us swim in the deep water because we have to pass the swim test. So we had to play in the mud water for babies. I wish I could go swimming in Josh's pool.

They made us eat gross food that Audrey likes. She likes yucky food that is made out of sea sponges and vegetables that you have never heard of.

I miss you.

Love,

Noah

"Are you writing to your parents?" Chip asked.

"Yeah." I was the only one still sitting up in my bed. Everyone else was trying to sleep.

"Lights out," Harrison barked. Then he put his pillow over his head.

I turned off my flashlight, and suddenly it was pitch dark.

"Did you tell them you wanted to stay?"

"I'm going to tell them tomorrow. Don't we get to call them tomorrow?"

"Yeah. What are you going to say tomorrow?"

"I'm not sure yet."

"Why? Don't you want to find the pirate treasure?"

"Yeah."

"Don't you want to find the Zombie Crow?"

I jumped at the thought of it. "No! Do you?"

"Stop talking," Harrison whined.

"We could solve the mystery," Chip said, ignoring Harrison.

"I don't know about that." I tucked myself deep into my covers. If the Zombie Crow was real, it probably wouldn't be a good idea to find it.

"What about toasting marshmallows?"

He had a point.

"What about Mudd Lake?" asked Harrison. "And tofu. And Crazy Alex."

"Be quiet, Harrison," Chip said, "I thought you didn't want people to talk."

Mikey was so asleep that he was snoring.

"Great," said Harrison.

"No, it's good," I said, "then we won't hear the Zombie Crow if he's on the roof again."

"That was a stick," Weatherman whispered loudly.

I didn't even know Weatherman was awake.

"Doesn't mean it's not out there," said Harrison.

"Whatever," said Chip. "this place is still way better than my house."

"Why? What's wrong with your house?" I couldn't imagine liking camp better than my own house.

"There's no place to play. And everybody goes away for the summer."

"Where's your house?"

"Boston."

"Oh, I live in Worcester."

"Hey! We're practically neighbors!"

"Isn't Boston like, an hour from Worcester?" asked Weatherman.

Chip sat up. "Yeah, okay, where are you from?"

"Brooklyn."

"Is that in New York?"

"Yes."

"Why isn't anybody asking me where I'm from?" Harrison whined.

"We thought you wanted everyone to stop talking," said Chip.

"Nashua, New Hampshire. Now everybody be quiet and go to sleep."

I didn't fall asleep right away. I was thinking about whether I wanted to go home or whether I wanted to stay at camp. I had this feeling I was missing out by not being at home. I was afraid my friends were doing fun things without me, and that my parents were having barbeques in the backyard, and the ice cream truck was driving down our street every other day, and I wasn't there to get my usual: rocket pop and a package of Razzles. I was afraid that what was happening back home was better than what was happening here at camp.

CHAPTER 14
THE LAKE MONSTER

In the morning, it was so foggy. It looked like the whole camp was in the clouds. We walked near the lake on the way to the main office, and that's when I saw it: a pointy black head bobbing up and down in the water!

"Look, you guys!" I screamed. "It's the creature!"

Everyone stopped in their tracks and looked out at the lake.

Even Dev stopped. "I don't see anything."

"I see it!" Mikey yelled.

We all ran toward the lake to get a better look.

But it was gone.

"Did you really see it, Mikey?" Chip asked as we got back on the path to the main office.

"Yeah! I saw something!"

"I saw it too," said Harrison.

I was excited that I wasn't the only one. "I told you!"

"Yeah," Harrison continued, "it had a big, red head with horns and big teeth."

"That's not funny," I said. "I really saw something."

"So did I," said Harrison.

"But I really did," I said, probably not loud enough for anyone to hear.

"What did you see, Mikey?" Dev asked.

"I saw a black thing going up and down and moving around in the water."

I looked at Mikey. "That's what I saw!"

"It could have been a tree branch," Dev said.

"But it was moving like it was alive!" Mikey declared.

"Yeah!" I shouted. (It could have been a tree branch, though.)

ॐ

We got to the office, and I had to wait in line to call my parents. I started getting nervous as if the future of the entire summer was riding on this phone call. The truth is, it kind of was. Should I stay at camp, or should I go home? Yes, I liked all the guys in my cabin, even Harrison. Sure, it was pretty nice being in a cabin deep in the forest. But there was no avoiding the Gray Wolves. Crazy Alex even said they would "have their revenge"—whatever that meant. I'm not sure I would ever get used to Audrey's food, and then there was the fact that I was always wondering if my parents were suddenly doing actual fun things, and I was missing it.

Should I stay at camp, or should I go? The answer to that question would mean the difference between a happy, fun summer, and the worst summer ever. I had to give the right answer.

"Hello? Mom? It's Noah."

"Hi, honey. How's camp?"

"It's okay."

Then my father got on the phone. "Hi, Noah. How's camp?"

"Okay," I said.

"Are you having fun?"

"Yeah."

"Did you decide if you want to stay or if you want us to come to get you?"

"I think so. Do you miss me?"

"We sure do," said Dad.

"Are you making friends?" Mom asked.

"Yeah."

"What have you learned so far? Did they teach you how to start a fire?" asked Dad.

"No."

"He's only been there a few days," said Mom.

"He was going to tell us if he wanted to stay at camp or if he wanted to come home," said Dad.

"Well," I said, turning around and looking at the guys playing tag outside the office door, "I really miss my bed, and my room, and Mom's food—"

"But you're such a picky eater," Mom interrupted.

"Julie, he was about to tell us if he wanted to stay at camp or not," said Dad.

"Yeah, I want to stay."

"We're so happy to hear that!" Mom and Dad both said.

"Don't you miss me?"

"We really miss you," said Dad. "We just want you to make the most of your summer."

The most would be finding the pirate treasure. But it would be a pretty good deal just doing stuff with my bunk.

"Time's up," Steve said, sticking his head into the office. "Harrison's turn to use the phone."

"Oh, okay. I have to hang up now."

"We love you!" my parents yelled in unison.

"I love you, too. Bye." It was hard to hang up. Now that I said I wanted to stay, camp suddenly felt different. Now I felt like I was officially a camper, not just a visitor at camp.

Mikey, Chip, and Weatherman gathered around me when I came out of the office.

"What'd you tell them?" Chip asked.

"I'm staying."

They all clapped and jumped around.

Chip put his hand on my shoulder. "We have a lot to get done this summer. By the way, you're it." He lifted his hand off and ran away.

Mikey let out a scream, and he and Weatherman ran in opposite directions.

Now I have to go tag one of them. What else am I going to do? I'm it.

THE END

ABOUT THE AUTHOR

C.K. Bushnell grew up on the east coast exploring the woods around her home and her grandparents' farm, uncovering ancient cellars hidden beneath the forest leaves, digging for buried treasure of old bottles from a time gone by, and searching for tadpoles and turtles in the swamp. Now on the west coast, C.K. continues to explore, not only the forests and mountains, but the mysterious mining towns of the Old West, and the Victorian houses hidden in plain sight on the busy city streets. Most of all, C.K. continues to imagine characters in places both familiar and unfamiliar, striving to be their best selves.

Made in the USA
Coppell, TX
07 June 2021